UNCHAINED

SHIFTER NIGHT

CHARLENE HARTNADY

UNCHAINED
Copyright February © 2018 by Charlene Hartnady
Cover art by Melody Simmons
Edited by KR
Website Updates and VA Simplicity

Proofread by Brigitte Billings (brigittebillings@gmail.com)
Produced in South Africa
charlene.hartnady@gmail.com

First Paperback Edition 2018

CHAPTER 1

There was a loud crash and Gage jumped to his feet. From dreaming about... he couldn't remember... to wide awake in an instant. His vision remained blurred with sleep for a half a second before he was able to focus.

"Ash," his voice was still croaky from disuse. There was an edge of confusion evident. His brother was breathing heavily. The male's eyes were wide, they held a wild edge. Gage could scent anger; that and the acrid smell of fear.

Sweat dripped from Ash's brow. "Get moving," he screamed, the muscles standing up on either side of his neck. "They have them!" His brother's face twisted with both anguish and disbelief as he shouted, "Those fuckers took my family!" Then he threw his head back and roared. A sound so deafening that Gage was forced to cover his ears with his hands.

Gage frowned. Half a dozen questions raced through

his mind all at once. "Who has them? By them, I'm assuming you mean Alice and the children?" He tried to keep his voice even and to remain calm despite the adrenaline that coursed through him.

Ash thread his fingers through his hair, fisting his hands. "Fuck!" he growled as he doubled over, still clutching his hair. "Oh my fuck!" The words were laced with anger and disbelief. There was more there though. He could hear the pain and utter devastation. "There is no time, we must leave now." The scent of fear grew stronger, almost choking him. He'd never seen his brother like this. *Never.* That was saying something since Ash had lost a mate and a child before.

Gage felt his heart-rate pickup. He reached for the jeans that lay discarded next to his still rumpled bed and tugged them on, one leg at a time. "Tell me what happened." There was still a rasp in his voice.

Ash was pacing the room, his eyes moving from left to right. His jaw was tightly clenched. "They're gone. When I came back outside, they were fucking gone. All four of them. Like they'd vanished into thin air." He sounded broken. Completely destroyed. His red-rimmed eyes glistened.

"Are you sure they didn't go for a walk or something? Maybe—"

"No!" Ash snarled. "Those fuckers took them. There was no scent trail. It was as if they disappeared into the ether. I know it was them. What the fuck do they want with my mate? With innocent children? The twins are still cubs. Ethan is a boy... just a little boy." His voice broke with emotion. Ash wiped at his eyes with frantic, angry swipes.

UNCHAINED

"Take me to where it happened."

"No!" Another loud snarl. "We have to go after them now." Again, his eyes darted around the room. His muscles bulged. His teeth were sharp. If he became any more agitated, Ash would shift. The male's fur would be just beneath the surface of his skin, prickling, his nail beds would be tingling. His gums would feel much the same. Then he snarled, turning on his heel. "I'm done talking. Done waiting." Ash roared again. This time, louder than before as he rushed for the door.

Gage grabbed his arm. He needed to talk some sense into the male. He could understand why his brother was so frantic, so out of his mind, but running off half-cocked was not going to solve anything.

Ash yanked himself free and headed out the door. This time when Gage gripped his arm, Ash turned and popped him one on the side of his jaw with a meaty thud. Dull pain exploded and he staggered back a few steps.

Four males stood a little ahead of Ash. Probably attracted by the noise. "Stop him!" Gage yelled but none of them moved.

Just then, Ward rounded the bend. The male lived next door so he no doubt heard the commotion. "What's going on?" He was frowning heavily.

"My family was taken." Ash's voice was deep and hoarse. So close to shifting that his muscles were thicker and roped. Even those of his throat.

Gage needed to talk some sense into him. "Go after them how? Where would we even start?" He couldn't begin to understand what was going through the male's head. Couldn't begin to understand what he was feeling.

"We have to do something! Please." He turned and

gripped Gage by the forearms and squeezed – hard. Any more pressure and his bones were going to snap. "We have to." His brother turned to Ward as he let go.

"Fuck!" Ward growled.

"Take us to where this happened. We need to try to figure this out. To figure them out. Maybe they left some sort of clue," Gage said.

"That's a good idea." Ward nodded.

"It happened right outside the house. Ethan wanted to play outside. The boys were napping in their stroller." Ash clenched and unclenched his fists. He spoke quickly. "I went back in to get us another cup of coffee and when I returned, they were gone. Gone!" he repeated the word, his eyes becoming wild, his face contorting in anguish once again. "The stroller too. Fucking gone! Like before, there was no scent. No prints. Nothing at all." Ash swallowed thickly, his Adam's apple bobbed. "It was just like when Meredith was taken." He ground his teeth. "Alice has been beside herself with worry and now she's gone too. What the fuck…" His brother wiped his eyes before the gathering wetness could fall. He sniffed hard.

Gage could remember that moment all too clearly since he had been with the human healer at the time of her abduction. The incident had taken place only five short days ago. The beast that had taken her was big, strong and faster than anything he'd seen before. He was lucky to be alive. "Sounds like it's them." There was no other explanation.

"Yes, it does." Ward's jaw was tight. His eyes bright. The male was probably thinking how it could have just as easily been his own family. "With all the extra scouting parties, this still happened." He shook his head.

"They're confident fucks."

Suddenly someone screamed and a loud snarl followed. The noise came from some distance. They all turned towards where the sound had come from. There was another blood-curdling scream and they took off, adrenaline pumping. Hackles raised.

CHAPTER 2

E dith looked down at the tiny infant in her lap. His skin was so incredibly soft. The little one was perfect in every way. From his gummy mouth to his itty bitty toes. "I can't believe he's already two months old," she gushed, glancing up at Ana. "Firstly, because he looks far too small to be anything other than a newborn," she paused to take in a breath, "and then secondly, because it took me this long to get out to see you."

Ana giggled. "Yeah, well, shifter babies are really small. You must remember that I was only pregnant for three months." She hooked a strand of blonde hair behind her ear.

"Nuts!" Edith shook her head. "I still can't believe it." She lifted her eyes in thought. "I suppose that it's a good thing. Rather get it over and done with as quickly as possible, right?"

"Right." Ana smiled. "Although," her expression

turned wistful, "I quite liked the whole experience. Maybe not the two weeks of nausea but other than that I really enjoyed being pregnant. Feeling my baby grow inside me. Feeling his little kicks. It was almost over before it began."

"I suppose you are right. I'm so sorry it took me so long to get my ass in gear and to get myself over here. It's just that Jeff has really been trying to move into my area. That's why I can't stay as long as I'd like. I have a show day next Sunday." The Jones property was one of those pieces of real-estate that you just knew would sell without too much hassle. Well-appointed, well maintained, lock up and go. It ticked all the boxes, including being north-facing and having river-frontage. There was nothing not to like, except, maybe the price tag, but the place was worth it, so it would sell regardless. Edith called that a serious win in her book, since she lived off commission. The only downside was that it was a dated house and – big sigh - she wished she could afford to buy it for herself. *Oh well!*

"Is that asshole still trying his luck?"

Jeff could go and suck eggs. He'd had his eye on her suburbs since he started at the agency two years ago. "Like you wouldn't believe it? And to think I taught him everything he knows. Little shit!"

"You're telling me. I don't miss the drama and the boring day-to-day stuff, but I sometimes do miss my old job." Ana took a sip of her tea.

"Seriously?" Edith shook her head. "If I had a hunk like Winston and lived out in this paradise... well, Jeff could take all of my properties. I wouldn't care. I sometimes get so sick of having to go it alone, you know?

What am I saying? You, of all people, know."

"I've told you a hundred times, your guy is out there somewhere."

Edith couldn't help but roll her eyes. It wasn't that she was a negative person. It really wasn't. She'd had enough though. She'd been on enough awful dates. Been hopeful too many times to count, and now she was done. Finished. She wasn't looking. She no longer believed in true love. She didn't want to settle on a mediocre relationship either, so…

"I can see by the look on your face that you don't believe me." Ana put her mug down with a clunk and the baby in her lap started.

Edith rocked her legs from side to side and Logan settled back down. "I guess I don't believe you," she sighed. "I tried my hand at finding love," A good couple of times, she thought to herself. "I failed. I'm going to get myself a cat or two and be done with it."

"That's ridiculous." Ana made a face. "You have to be open to the possibility or love might be staring you right in the face and you won't even see it."

"Doubtful at best," Edith laughed. It came out sounding a bit strained. Oh well, it was the line of conversation. Best she move away from talk of men and love. *Arghhh!* It was giving her a headache. "So," she carefully picked up her own mug, trying not to jostle the baby, "why was my trip nearly canceled anyway?" Ana had messaged her to say it was potentially off and then, just yesterday, she'd said that it was back on.

"I had to beg to get them to agree to let you come. You see, a woman was kidnapped a couple of days ago. A human, visiting the village."

Edith felt her mouth drop open. "What do you mean kidnapped? How? Why?"

Ana shrugged, her eyes were wide. If Edith didn't know any better, she would say that her friend was afraid. "We're not sure. Some or other creature or creatures that live in these woods." Ana seemed to look around them, like she was imagining herself deep in the forest.

"A creature?" Edith sounded skeptical. She couldn't help it; it sounded a bit far-fetched. Then again, she was visiting a shifter village in the middle of nowhere. Anything was possible after that, right?

Ana nodded. "We've seen signs of them… it. We're not sure but we think there are more than one. One of them left a large footprint. There have been two attacks. Once on one of the Alphas. It was Winston's Alpha, he was there when it happened. Ward was badly injured. The Alpha didn't see much, but someone," she paused, "some*thing*, tore into Ward that day. His injuries were severe. Then, a couple of days ago, one of the bear shifters was torn up really badly and the woman he was with was taken."

"No shit!"

"I wouldn't joke about a thing like this. Gage said it was huge and powerful. He said it was ridiculously fast despite its size as well. We also know that the creature is winged; Gage – the guy who was attacked – saw that much but nothing else. That's why they almost canceled your trip. Since we're staying indoors, I didn't think you'd be in any danger."

Edith snorted. "Winged? Really? Maybe he hit his head a little too hard." She could only hope. This creature sounded surreal. Surely the shifter, Gage, had banged his head a little too hard or something?

Ana swallowed the large gulp of tea she had just taken. "Nope, it's the only explanation. How else could they come and go without leaving any prints? He definitely saw wings, and they were feathered. The one and only print they've left to date was," she widened her eyes, "huge and looked to be feline." She frowned. "It doesn't make any sense."

That sparked some sort of memory. *Oh yes!* Her younger brother went through a phase where he couldn't get enough of mythological creatures. Anything from Bigfoot to the Kraken and everything in-between. "That's interesting." Edith licked her lips. "I think I have a picture of what this creature might be. In theory anyway." It so couldn't be what she was thinking though. A creature like that simply didn't exist outside of books and fairytales. Did it?

Ana frowned. "Oh! Okay. What did you have in mind?"

She may as well share her thoughts. "Well, you know how Tommy—"

"Quiet!" The look that came over Ana's face was nothing short of scary. She held up a hand, her face turning panicked in an instant. Then, her best friend leaned over and took her son from Edith, holding the baby to her chest.

"What is it?" Edith finally asked, whispering.

Ana shook her head. "I'm not sure. I heard screaming."

"I didn't hear anything."

"My hearing has improved since mating with

Winston. I definitely heard it and it sounded bad… really bad. Something terrible has happened." She rocked the baby, her eyes wide, her face deathly pale.

CHAPTER 3

Everyone in the room spoke at once. The females and children huddled together, whispering amongst themselves. Quietly reassuring each other.

There were many who argued and there were also those who were in all-out panic mode. Screaming and ranting, as if that would solve anything. Then there were those, like himself, who stood in shocked silence. Gage let his eyes move across the room, coming to rest on the latest victim. Calum's face was a riot of blues, purples and greens. One of his eyes was swollen shut. His lip was scabbed over where it had burst open from the impact. All in all, he had gotten away lightly. Gage had taken a full day to recover. Whereas Calum, barely an hour after he was knocked unconscious, was already able to function. "What are we going to do about this?" the agitated male snarled. "What the fuck just happened?" There were blood spatters down his chest and dirt stains on the front of his jeans.

Ash paced back and forth, muscles bulging, still halfway to a shift. Gage could see that his brother was barely holding it together.

"Silence," Ward commanded – and not for the first time. "Silence," he repeated, louder this time. Then he snarled; the vicious call echoed around the room, it demanded instant obedience and submission. Ward was an Alpha, he had that inherent ability, just like others of his stature.

Almost everyone did as they were commanded. Though there were one or two Alphas who continued to talk quietly amongst themselves, able to ignore the tone of a fellow leader. Ash continued to pace.

"Is everyone present?" Ward asked, then looked around the dining hall. It was the largest room in the village. Most of the tables and chairs had been carried out to make space for everyone. Females with young children sat on the chairs along the walls.

There were murmurs of agreement.

"We need to do something and fast," Ash rasped, his voice guttural. His vocal cords had thickened, more like those of a bear than a human.

"Agreed." Ward nodded, he looked from Calum to Ash and back again.

"I want my Annie back. As you know, she is with child." Calum's eyes turned pleading. His voice was thick with emotion. "What do they want with a mated female?" He shook his head.

"What do they want with innocent children and cubs?" Ash growled out each word, his eyes dark.

"We don't know, and we're not going to waste time guessing. Are you sure you didn't see anything?" Ward addressed Calum. He then looked around the room, thick with bodies huddled close. "That none of you saw anything?"

Calum shook his head. "The bastard was too quick. I was out before I even hit the ground." He looked defeated.

"I didn't see a thing," one of the mated human females stated. "I found him lying there and screamed. I just knew something awful had happened."

"I heard the scream," another female said. She shrugged. "Although I'm right across the road from where it happened, I didn't see anything and neither did Jake." She clutched her son tighter to her side. The boy was eight, if Gage could remember correctly. The female grimaced. "It's frightening to think that this could've happened to any one of us. It might still—"

"No!" Ward shook his head. "There will be safety in numbers. "We have to band together. Put guards on watch."

"What about Alice and my cubs?" *Shit!* It looked like Ash's jaw was slightly elongated. His eyes were blazing, his hands clenched tight at his sides. Every muscle was roped and ready.

"We'll have to send out scouting parties to try to find those who are missing." It was the panther Alpha, Brock.

"Agreed," Ward chimed in. "We can't just do nothing."

"Damned straight," Calum growled. "I need my female back. We have to find her." Worry lines were etched into his forehead and around his mouth.

"I'm heading up one of the parties." Ash looked like he was ready to fight anyone who tried to say differently.

"Absolutely," Ward said, "but you will need a couple of strong males and one of the Seconds at your side." Ash wouldn't be thinking too clearly right now, he needed all the help he could get.

Winston stepped forward just as Gage did the same. The male's head was bowed and he was frowning heavily. "I wish I could be with you on this one." Winston shook his head slowly from side to side.

"You stay with Ana and your pup. They need you right now," Ash said.

"I'd be honored to join your team as second in command." Gage loved his nephews and had a good relationship with Alice, Ash's mate. The thought of anything happening to any one of them left him cold. The thought of something happening to little Ethan… his heart beat faster.

Edith knew that she should be afraid. It was hard to feel any kind of nervousness surrounded by so many huge guys. Even with all of their emotions running high.

"I'd be honored to join your team as second in command," one of the two giant shifter-men said. They looked very similar. So much so that Edith was convinced they were twins. Brothers at the very least. The one who was pacing was scary looking. Ana had filled her in on how his family had been abducted along with another woman. She felt for the two men. Could see that they were in a really bad way. Could see it in their eyes, their faces. Anger, sadness, frustration – it was all there, easy to read.

"I'm sorry." The other big, dark-haired guy with the vivid green eyes put up one of his hands. According to

Ana, he was the wolf Alpha. She couldn't remember his name. "I can't allow you to join Ash's scout team." He turned to another guy. This one had long, gleaming hair that most women would die to have. "Brock," he addressed the panther Alpha – another titbit from Ana – who inclined his head. "Can your Second go with Ash?" Ward asked.

"Wait a minute," the less scary of the two who looked like brothers interrupted. "Why can't I go? My brother needs me." So, they *were* related. Edith had guessed correctly. They really were almost identical looking, so it was no wonder.

"I need you to assist on another task." The wolf Alpha turned slightly, locking eyes with her. Edith felt her back press up against the chair. She was tempted to look behind her but knew there would be no one there since she was up against the wall. Surely he didn't mean to focus on her? "I'm afraid we need to cut your trip short, human."

Shit! So, he *was* addressing her. She had a mini-panic session when everyone focused on her. *Pay attention, Edith! What had he just said?* Oh, that she had to go back to Sweetwater. Without waiting for her response – it was obviously more of a statement than a question – he continued. "It's not safe for you here. I don't believe whoever did this knows you are here or they may have taken you. Females are clearly high on their list though."

"I understand," she said simply. What else could she say? She was a guest here. This was their turf. Edith hated the idea of cutting her trip short, but it made sense.

Ana reached over and squeezed her hand before letting it go. Edith glanced at her friend. Ana gave her a baleful look. Edith mouthed '*sorry.*' Ana shrugged and then gave a small nod, as if to say that she understood as well. It didn't make it any easier. They'd both been looking forward to this visit for so long.

The wolf Alpha turned back to the calmer of the two brothers. Edith got a really good look at the guy; he was huge, one of the biggest shifters in the room and he did not look impressed. Heavy frown lines creased his forehead. The faded t-shirt he was wearing pulled tight across his chest. In any other situation, she might have checked him out. "What could possibly be more important than rescuing my nephews and my brother's mate?"

"I need you to command the team that takes the human back to Sweetwater. You're strong and, despite being a bear, you're fast. This mission requires a cool head. The team must move quickly and quietly. I want you gone within half an hour."

"No!" The guy shook his head, looking incredulous. "No way!" he added, his voice rough and deep. Then he pulled in a deep breath. It looked like he was trying to calm himself down. "You can't blame me after what happened. I lost a female five days ago." So, he was the one who was attacked when that woman was abducted. "I'm not the right person for this detail."

Great! That instilled serious confidence. Edith licked her lips, trying to stay calm.

"That's another reason I think you're perfectly suited to this mission. You've seen one of these beasts. You know what it's capable of. I know you won't underestimate the situation."

"Ward is right." It was the brother. "Get the female

safely home and then guard our females and children until I return."

The guy looked at his brother for a long while before finally nodding. "I don't like it," he mumbled under his breath. It certainly didn't inspire much confidence in her. Should she be worried at this point? It seemed like it. Butterflies jostled about in her belly and her mouth felt dry.

"Thank you." The wolf Alpha touched him on the side of his arm, giving him a tight smile. "Take six males along with you."

"Only six?" His dark eyes widened, and his mouth dropped open for a second or two.

"Yes." The Alpha nodded. "Any more and you'll draw attention to yourselves. You need to move quickly and quietly."

The guy's jaw clenched tight for a moment and then he nodded once, shoving his hands into his pockets.

"Choose your six males and head out now," the wolf Alpha barked out. "Human," he looked at her, "pack quickly. You have ten minutes to get your things together. Once this situation has been taken care of, you are welcome to return."

"Wait for a second," Ana piped up. "Edith had an idea of what might be doing this."

All the eyes in the room moved back to her. Edith tried not to squirm in her seat. She swallowed hard. "It's just a theory. A... a guess, that's all."

"You seemed like you had a good idea earlier when we were discussing it," Ana said.

"It's simply a theory based on the feline paw print and the feathered wings," she spoke quickly. "It's nothing.

Forget about it."

Ward folded his arms. "No, I'd like to hear this theory if you make it really quick. Until now, no one has had even the slightest clue what this creature could be."

"Okay." Edith swallowed thickly, trying to remain calm under so much scrutiny. "My younger brother has always had a love for mythological creatures."

"Mythological creatures?" The guy assigned to lead the team that would take her back home, snorted. He even rolled his eyes. "We don't have time for this."

"Let's hear the human out," Ward addressed the guy before turning back to her. "Make it quick, human," Ward instructed.

"Edith," she cleared her throat. "My name is Edith. Like I was saying, my brother, he was into creatures like Bigfoot and the Kraken. One of his favorites was the griffin. It has the body of a lion and the head of an eagle."

"Do you know anything about this creature?" Ward asked.

Edith pushed out a breath, trying to remember. "Um… it was one of Tommy's favorites because the griffin is considered to be king of all the creatures. They're supposed to be powerful and majestic creatures." She scrunched her eyes up in thought. "I think they have some kind of magic power, but I might be wrong."

The big shifter she'd come to think of as '*the asshole*' snorted out a laugh. "Magic, really?" He looked at her like she'd just developed a neon '*I'm crazy*' sign on her forehead.

Ward ignored him. "Anything else?" He kept his eyes firmly on her.

She decided to ignore him as well and turned her eyes

up in thought, coming up blank. She shook her head. "Nope, that's all I can remember."

The asshole rolled his eyes and blew out a breath through his nose. "Winged lion birds with magic powers. If it turns out to be true, I'll roast my dick on an open fire."

There were one or two snickers, but they quickly died down.

"Thank you for the information... hu— Edith. Safe travels!" Ward turned back to the gathering. They didn't believe her. She couldn't blame them. The whole thing was seriously far-fetched. Ward went on. "We will now discuss the scouting parties as well as sleeping arrangements and security details going forward."

"Safety in numbers is going to be important," the panther Alpha said.

A big hulk of a man stepped in front of her, blocking her view of the room. Make that, blocking out everything. It was him. The asshole. He leaned down. "We need to go. Now." Such a deep, masculine voice. Built like a brick shithouse as well, but without having that overblown look. She was momentarily stunned. His eyes had these golden flecks around the irises. His hair wasn't black, just very dark brown. His jaw was as manly as it got. Strong like the rest of him and covered in light stubble. It was his biceps that had her mesmerized though. Thick and hard. "I said now," he added, his voice a soft, deep vibration. He leaned in and picked her up off of the chair. As in right up... her feet dangled off the floor and he hadn't even broken a sweat. There was nary a grimace on his face either. "Put me down," she whispered.

"Quiet," he whispered back.

The meeting was in full swing. If she made a ruckus, they would interrupt.

To make matters worse, the asshole smelled really good. Like obscenely good. He began to walk, taking big strides. She waved to Ana and mouthed '*bye*' since the two remaining Alphas seemed to be having a heated debate on whether to stick together or to break up into three groups.

"You can put me down now," she said as the door to the dining hall swung closed behind them.

He flat out ignored her and continued walking.

"I can walk, you know."

He continued to ignore her, tightening his hold on her.

"Hey!" she added, with far less conviction. Edith sighed as she clutched his shoulders. His very broad, well-muscled shoulders. She'd forgotten how buff shifters were. It had been months since she and Jacob had spent that night together. Jacob had been really cute and really big, but nothing compared to this. This was next level. It was such a pity that most shifters seemed to be fixated on one thing and one thing only. This one just happened to be a big fat jerk as well.

CHAPTER 4

G age paced outside Ana and Winston's place. Three wolf shifters were on guard at the rear of the building and three were standing only a few meters in front of him. He'd been acting like a dick to the human. He needed to try to ease up. What had happened to Meredith five days ago was not this female's fault. The feelings of guilt and anxiety that coursed through him were not her doing. This whole shitty situation had zero to do with her. She was most likely really nervous, and with good cause. Gage was going to be polite to her going forward. Unless of course her life was in danger, or unless she was doing something that might cause her life to be in danger, and then, all bets were off.

Where the hell was she?

Calm down, Gage! Calm down!

The human finally... fucking finally... came outside, dragging a large suitcase behind her. "What the fuck are you wearing?" he snapped. It couldn't be helped. Then he caught a whiff of her. *Holy shit!* "What's that smell?" He sniffed.

Her eyes widened in clear disbelief. "What do you mean what am I wearing? Shorts and a top."

"They're too short." He allowed his gaze to roam her lush thighs. Lush hips, lush fucking everything, he thought as his eyes settled on her plump breasts. "That top won't work either."

"It's seriously hot. There's nothing wrong with shorts and a spaghetti strap top. I'm wearing sunscreen – all over – so it's all good. I wore something similar on the way in this morning." She shrugged like it was no biggie. This female had no fucking clue.

"Sunblock. So that's the smell then." He bit back a growl. Did this human want to die? Then again, there were some things worse than death. If she was captured, she would be in deep trouble. He tried not to think about it. Steering his thoughts along that path would make him think of Alice and little Ethan. Of the twins. Of the other two females who had been taken. Anger and frustration ate at him.

"Smell?" She sniffed her underarms. "I showered not so long ago. I used shower gel and everything. I'm not sure what you mean." Her eyes were wide.

"You need to shower again. You have two minutes. I'm coming in with you." He began to usher her back towards the door.

"What?" Her eyes were wide. "As in… in the shower with me? There's no way —"

"No, not in the shower, in the house." He glanced back at the three males; despite the circumstances, they looked amused.

"Oh," she sighed with what seemed like relief and then turned and entered the house.

"This time, after you're finished, no creams, no lotions or deodorants of any kind. No perfume or sunblock. Shifters have a fantastic sense of smell and I'm sure these creatures do too. Cover your legs and arms, we will be moving at a fast pace and may need to flee. I don't want your pretty skin to get scratched up."

Pretty.

What the fuck was that all about?

"Oh!" She blinked a couple of times. "I didn't think of any of that. I guess I've never been in danger before, although this is just a precaution, right?" She didn't wait for him to answer. "I guess covering up makes sense." She turned towards the hall.

"Oh, and human…"

"Edith." She glanced back, still moving, only much slower than before.

Shit! He was supposed to be polite and here he was blowing the whole damned thing. Her safety came first though. She needed to know that he was serious. "Edith," he said.

"Yes?"

"Come back out after your shower in your underwear."

She stopped walking and turned back to him; Gage hadn't known that humans could move that quickly. She spun on her heel. There was a look of confusion on her face. "Why the heck would I do that?" She planted her hands on her ample hips and thrust out her succulent breasts.

Breasts that were made for a male to snuggle into and

maybe never come up for air, period. *Head out of the gutter, Gage!* It had been nearly two months since his last trip to Sweetwater. Two very long months – excuse the pun – *hard* months. He was a male after all. One with a job to do. "It's not like that. I need to get my scent on you. All over you."

Edith shook her head so hard her curls bounced. She scrunched up her cute-as-a-button nose. "I'm not sure what that means exactly but I'm *not* game."

"You scent of sweet, delicious human. Those creatures will be drawn to you like a homing beacon. If I was you, I'd be afraid and doing everything I was told. I'm trying to help you, Edith."

She gulped and he picked up the bitter scent of fear. Damn, it wasn't how he wanted this to go. She finally nodded once. "Okay, but don't get any ideas."

"Believe me I won't." He held up both hands. "Please be as quick as you can. Two minutes max."

"I'll do my best." She disappeared down the hall.

Gage huffed out a pent-up breath and ran a hand through his hair. *Why me?* He instantly regretted his thoughts. He wasn't usually prone to pity parties. With everything going on around them, taking the human back to Sweetwater was nothing in comparison. He wasn't missing a mate or a child or all of the above. It still didn't mean that he wanted this assignment. What if something happened to the female? What if…? He groaned. He couldn't think like this. Gage needed to force himself to put a positive spin on this situation. If it came to it, and he hoped to god it didn't, but if it did, then he was going to do everything in his power to protect the human. He would lay down his own life, before losing her to those creatures. The bastards had to be evil. There was no other way around it. Who abducted pregnant females and such tiny cubs? Gage suppressed a growl.

Everyone would have to work together tirelessly. Whether wolves, bears or panthers. Ward had already sent word to the other ten packs. It would take a half a day to reach them with the news though. He wondered if they had been targeted too. He sure as hell hoped not!

He heard the female's approach and almost fell on his ass as she walked into the room. Gage cleared his throat and forced his eyes onto hers. *Shit!* Her cheeks were pink. By the look in her eyes and the way she was trying to shield her lace-clad breasts, he could see that she was self-conscious. No wonder. The ensemble left little to the imagination.

Fuck! White lace. Thin, translucent and mouthwatering. He wasn't looking though. Not at her puckered nipples. Not at the flesh that was spilling over the top of the cups. Certainly not at the lace-covered snatch of fur between those heavenly thighs. This female wasn't just tits and ass; she was hips, thighs and everything in-between.

He cleared his throat a second time. "Maybe you would be more comfortable wearing a t-shirt." There was no way he could get through putting his scent on her without putting his dick inside her too. Deep inside. Not with her looking like that. This was no time to think of sex. *Stop, Gage! Just stop!*

She nodded and leaned over her bag. He almost groaned out loud. That ass! Oh, that ass! Two globes of utter perfection bobbed up and down as she pulled on the zipper. His hands itched to squeeze and fondle.

He turned away from her instead, listening to her open the bag and then dig around in it.

"Okay, all done," she announced.

He turned back. The shirt wasn't as big as he had hoped but it covered enough of her to allow him to think more clearly. "I think a bed would work best."

Her eyes widened, and her mouth dropped open.

He quickly went on. "I'm going to rub myself up against you, front and back. It will be easier on a large flat surface. We can do it right here on the floor, I merely thought that a bed might be more comfortable for you." Her eyes widened even more. Gage held up a hand, hoping to calm her. They didn't have time for this shit. "You're welcome to rub up on me if you would prefer." *What the hell was he doing to himself?* "If this wasn't necessary, I wouldn't have brought it up. You just smell that good." It was true, she did. So very sweet and delicious. Like chocolate-dipped honeycomb.

She finally sucked in a deep breath and nodded. "Okay. Follow me." Edith led him through to a bedroom. From the scent – or lack thereof – he could tell that it was the spare room.

The female looked apprehensive as she lay down. Her chest heaved.

"Don't be nervous. We'll be done in half a minute." He needed to respect this female. Needed to dial back on these dirty thoughts. Needed to stop thinking of her as the sum of her really magnificent body parts. He was not going to allow himself to become aroused. No damned way. Time was a-wasting here. He needed to keep his mind clear and in the game.

The mattress dipped as he climbed onto the bed.

Thank fuck he was wearing jeans.

"You were an asshole back there." She looked him head-on. Her eyes were actually more green than brown. Not striking in any way but really pretty. Especially considering how big they were. Framed by long, thick black lashes.

Direct. He liked that. Big time. "I'm sorry. I guess I was a bit of an asshole. The whole mythical creature thing sounded pretty far-fetched though."

"I said it was a theory. I made it very clear that I wasn't sure. Hearing the description of these creatures sparked a memory. You didn't have to be so… nasty."

"I said that I was sorry, and I meant it. We're under a lot of pressure here." He looked down at her legs. Soft, lush, smooth skin. Very fucking sexy. Not that he was looking. "I'm going to start with your feet. I need to touch you… a lot. Don't hit me or kick me."

"Stay away from my… private parts and we'll be fine."

CHAPTER 5

The sexy asshole glanced up, his dark eyes giving nothing away. "I'll do my level best." He pulled off his shirt, tossing it next to the bed. Her mouth went more than a little dry. *Wowza! Holy freaking macaroni!* Talk about wide shoulders and pecs that could bounce shit off of them. Hell, she was sure that he could bounce her with one of those babies. And his abs. Oh, sweet baby Jesus, those abs. She only wished she could unsnap his jeans so that she could see them all. All three pairs of prime real estate. Just sitting there, waiting to be staked and claimed.

This wasn't supposed to be fun. In fact, she was supposed to hate this. She was *going* to hate this, dammit. He was about to get all touchy-feely with her. At least she got the impression that he wouldn't be doing this unless he really had to.

He picked up her feet and ran his hands over them. Edith tried hard to hold it in, even squirmed a little. In the end, she giggled. There was no stopping that baby when it burst out of her.

His gaze snapped back to hers and his hands stilled.

She raised her brows by way of apology. "I guess I'm a little ticklish."

He nodded once, moving to her calves using long, firm strokes. It was almost clinical and undoubtedly no-nonsense. It was silly, she hadn't wanted this, had been really nervous about it. Now that it was happening though, she kind of wished he would show some sort of enjoyment. All women enjoyed feeling sexy and wanted. Did she want to have sex with him? *No!* Not after what happened with Jacob. She wasn't a one-night-stand kind of girl. Sex wasn't just sex to her. It was something intimate and special, and like it or not, she attached feelings to the act. Having said that, it would be nice if he showed some sort of attraction or interest or something. Instead, she got nothing. Then again, look at him. *Just look!* He must have women throwing themselves at him at every turn. Why was she even thinking about sex? Maybe because a gorgeous guy was touching her. This was crazy. She needed to clear her mind.

"I need you to part your thighs a little." His voice was really deep and gravelly, but she didn't think it had anything to do with her. Then she registered what he had said. Her heart went to her throat.

"I need to get my scent all over you," he finally explained when she didn't respond.

"No looking, okay?" She raised her brows.

His jaw tightened. "Wouldn't dream of it." He looked like he meant it. She wasn't sure whether to be happy or sad.

Happy.

Definitely happy!

"Before you start groping me…" Why had she said that? It wasn't like that. "Um… you know what I mean?" She cleared her throat. "I don't even know your name."

"It's Gage, and I promise not to be inappropriate in any way."

Pity.

She bit her tongue, because for a moment, she almost said it out loud, which was crazy since he was about to take her on a perilous journey home. Since nothing about this whole situation was normal or nice in any way. Or it shouldn't be nice. He was such a hunk though. *Stop!* It was all just the nerves talking. "Okay," she said when she realized that he was waiting for an acknowledgment. "Good to meet you, Gage."

He didn't say anything.

Asshole.

Using the same firm strokes, he rubbed her up and down her thighs, even using his chest a little as well. *Oh goodness!* So hard. So darned masculine, even though the vast expanse of his torso was hairless and smooth. There was a smattering of black hair from his bellybutton which disappeared into those snug-fitting jeans. *Not thinking about that!*

"Still okay?"

She nodded. He pushed her legs back down and moved his big body over her. Only a couple of inches above her but not touching her in any way. Her breathing hitched. How could it not? Six and a half feet of pure muscle was poised above her. Those golden flecks around his irises made his eyes really beautiful. They were locked with hers. This whole moment felt oddly intimate even though it wasn't. Not even close.

"Pull up your shirt for me."

She sucked in a breath, wanting to argue but stopped herself. He didn't look in the least bit aroused or interested. He was doing this to help her. As a favor. He was ultimately doing his duty. Edith licked her lips and tugged up her shirt until it was just covering her boobs.

"Is it all the way up?" he asked, not breaking contact with her eyes for a moment.

She shook her head.

"Needs to be all the way," he said, looking bored.

She pulled it up further, until the material was bunched under her armpits, and then nodded. "Yes," she said the word on a huff.

"I'm sorry about this," Gage said as he lowered himself. Then hot, heavy male rubbed up against her. All his hard planes against her soft, curvy ones. It somehow almost felt right, yet very, very wrong.

She lifted her eyes to the ceiling, biting on her bottom lip to hold back a moan. Her nipples decided they liked the attention. The hard, hot friction. This, despite the situation they were in, and the fact that she didn't know this shifter from Adam. Would he be able to feel her pebbled flesh? She hoped not.

Gage lifted himself. "Turn around," he instructed.

Her cheeks burned, she avoided eye contact and moved onto her belly.

His chest vibrated as it connected with her back. He made what sounded like a growl. Soft, but angry. Was he angry? If so, why? His jeans abraded her ass and legs.

She tried not to think about it too much. Just kept her eyes squeezed shut. Tried not to enjoy it, even though she was embarrassed to her core. *Note to self, buy a set of full, cotton underwear for this type of situation.* Hopefully it never happened again. A lace G-string and lacy bra were not going to cut it for activities like this.

Then he was lifting himself off of her. "Get dressed," Gage commanded as he got back up. She noticed that he left the shirt lying right there on the floor. "Long pants, closed shoes and a long-sleeved shirt. I'd prefer it if that shirt stayed on as well. It has my scent on it." He glanced at her chest and straight back up, locking with her eyes. "We're at least fifteen minutes behind schedule, so I would appreciate it if you could be really quick. No perfume or any of that other stuff."

"Got it." Apprehension coiled within her. "Am I really in that much danger?"

He clenched his jaw.

"I mean, it can't be that bad, can it?" She heard the hesitancy in her own voice. Had she underestimated how much danger she was in?

Gage didn't say anything, which spoke volumes. "Oh shit!" Up until this moment, she'd somehow convinced herself that this was just a precaution. That all would be well. She'd been an idiot. Done the whole 'bury her head in the sand' thing. She was good at that.

"I'll take care of you, Edith. Of that, you can be certain."

"Like you took care of that other woman?" It came out before she could stop it. It was a terrible thing to say. Edith instantly regretted it. She covered her mouth with her hand. It wasn't like she could unsay it.

His eyes darkened.

"I'm sorry, I guess I'm just really nervous. I—"

"I deeply regret what happened to the human. That she was taken, but rest assured that I will protect you," Gage said with more conviction. "All of us will. Now get dressed and let's head out."

She swallowed thickly. "I'm really sorr—"

"It's fine!" By the frown he was sporting, she could see that it wasn't. "We need to get going."

Three minutes later, Gage zipped up her bag while she tied the laces on her sneakers. Then they were heading out.

Three guys moved into position in front of them, and by the sound of footfalls, there were a couple of guys behind them as well. They walked for two minutes. Gage carried her bag, making it look like it weighed nothing. She had to half-jog, half-walk to keep up with them. *Note to self, take some fitness classes.* Edith was a little out of breath by the time they made it to the forest edge.

The guys behind them moved in. She was shocked to see Jacob amongst the group. He gave her a quick smile. "Hi!"

"Hello." She tried to smile back, it probably looked more like a grimace. *Flip!* She hadn't expected to see him so up close and personal. Truth be told, she hadn't expected him to even acknowledge her. It had been a couple of months since she had last seen him.

"Do you two know one another?" Gage was frowning heavily.

Jacob nodded. "Yes." He grinned. "We're friends." He winked at her. It felt flirty. She was probably misreading the whole thing.

Edith had to hold back a groan and an eye roll. Moreover, she had to hold back an explanation about how she knew Jacob. *Oh, she could imagine herself saying, we had sex once and chatted a couple of times after that, but it was nothing.* It was nobody's business though, so she didn't elaborate.

She could see the wheels turning in Gage's brain. Could see him put two and two together. "Is this going to be a problem?" Gage looked agitated. "Is it going to get in the way of things?"

"No. Not at all," Jacob quickly answered, shaking his head. That grin was still firmly in place.

Of course not. What had gone down between them was nothing. Less than nothing. Just sex. "No!" she blurted, her voice a bit shrill. "No problem!" she added unnecessarily. She wanted to say a whole lot more but forced herself to keep quiet.

"Good." He narrowed his eyes on Jacob, ignoring her. "We stick together," he addressed the group, looking from one shifter to the next. "We need to move as fast as we can, taking the human into consideration. No sound." He turned to her. "Not a word. Is that understood?"

They all nodded. She did too when Gage looked pointedly at her. "Good." He looked at a sandy-haired guy. "Sawyer, you take the human's bag. Nathan, you strap it to his back."

The two men in question unsnapped their jeans. She'd forgotten about this part. She felt her eyes widen and looked away as they pulled their jeans off. "I would be happy to carry Edith," Jacob said, "we're friends."

She looked his way and he winked at her again. Winked. What? It definitely seemed like he was flirting with her. Their fling – hook-up was a better word – had happened months and months ago. She'd gone back to the Dark Horse several times and had talked to him, hoping something would come of it, but he hadn't been interested. Surely, he wasn't interested now?

"I will carry the human," Gage said. The whole sentence sounded more like a growl than words. "You focus on the job at hand."

Jacob instantly sobered and nodded once before unsnapping his jeans. Where to look? Where to… *Flip! Flip! Oh heck!* Gage pulled his jeans down his thighs. His… man part… was impressive despite not being hard. More than impressive, actually. Long and thick, hanging slightly to the right. Edith took a sharp breath, she tried to look away but couldn't. Gage was tanned, all over. She was right about those lower abs – impressive didn't come close to cutting it. There was also that whole V-thing he had going on. Gage turned a smidgen, giving her a glimpse of his ass. Yummy! Oh so very yummy! Also tanned and buff and… She forced herself to close her mouth and to stop drooling.

What was she doing ogling him? Her life could very well be in danger and she was checking him out. Just to the left of her, a guy she had slept with, had casual sex with, was naked as well. *What the hell!* She needed to stop this. She wasn't some giggling, horny teenage girl.

The sound of cracking filled the clearing and she watched in complete and utter fascination as Gage changed into a bear. A big, bristling grizzly bear. Every instinct told her to run and her heartrate picked up a whole lot. The shifters who had brought her here were wolves. Not nearly as intimidating.

She continued to stare. Those teeth were long and sharp. He was enormous, bigger than an actual bear. Not that she'd seen an actual bear this close, but he had to be bigger. Surely. Even though his body was covered in thick fur, she could tell he was well-muscled. His eyes, oh yeah, those were all Gage. The same dark brown with generous flecks of gold. Very beautiful. She realized with a start that he was laying down flat on his belly, making these growling noises.

He looked at her. Clearly trying to get her to hop on board. She walked over and gripped a handful of surprisingly soft fur. Sucking in a deep breath, she clambered up. Her legs were wide as she straddled him. Four wolves and two sleek panthers looked back at her. One of the wolves had her bag strapped to his back. It reminded her of just this morning.

Gage made a rumbling bear noise and began to walk. Slowly at first but quickly picking up the pace. She had to hold on tight, gripping with her hands and her legs.

Before long, they were racing. Screw this unknown creature, at this rate she might just die from a fall. It was a long way down. Edith pressed her lips together and concentrated on holding on for dear life.

CHAPTER 6

A ny faster and they would put the human in danger. Gage tried hard to keep his gait as even as possible. Fact of the matter was that bears lumbered. Even fast-moving bears. It was rocky and would be difficult for her to sit. The female would have been more comfortable riding on one of the others.

Tough shit! There was only one way to truly keep her safe and that was to keep her close. They headed through the thick undergrowth. He was careful not to turn too sharply and slowed whenever he needed to leap over a boulder or a fallen tree. It impressed him that the human didn't complain. Not a word, just as he had instructed. She was afraid. The bitter scent still lingered on her skin.

After about a half an hour they hit the open plain. Gage gave a soft growl, indicating that they should pick up the pace. The female's grip on his fur tightened. As did the clutching of her thighs. She made a tiny squeaking noise, more than likely struggling to hold on.

This couldn't be helped though. Gage wished he could reassure her, but there was no time. There had been two options, skirt around the plain and add an hour to their journey or risk the five or six minutes it would take to cross it. His back prickled. On more than one occasion, one of the males glanced upwards. It wasn't ideal, but unfortunately they didn't have a choice. The human would not be able to manage an extra hour. The journey was too tiring on a human female. It would have meant stopping to allow for a break, which was just as dangerous, if not more so, as risking crossing the plain. Gage concentrated on moving forward. On putting one foot in front of the other.

Two things happened.

There was a sharp stinging on his back and a shadow befell them. The stinging, he would later realize, was his fur being yanked out by the roots as the human tried to hold on. It was ultimately the shadow that gave it away. A sudden shadow appearing in the middle of an open plain?

Not possible

There was no time for thought. Gage leapt up, sinking his claws into its underbelly just as it shot up into the sky. Using every ounce of strength he possessed, Gage hung on and for all he was worth. They were moving so fast, he had to close his eyes. So quickly his stomach lurched and for a second he thought he might pass out. He clenched his teeth, holding back an almighty roar. If this beast knew he was there, it gave no indication, despite the fact that his claws were buried in its flesh. Strange thing was that it didn't seem to be bleeding. He couldn't smell blood. Couldn't feel it flowing onto his paws.

The thing suddenly slowed down a smidgen. He didn't have much strength left. It took all of his concentration to hold on. This would be much easier in human form. Then he was slipping... slipping. If he fell from this height, it would be game over. He'd look like ground beef. There was no regenerating from that.

His arms were shaking, his shoulders too. For once in his life, he cursed his bulk. In this instance, it was a hindrance. There was no way he could hold on while staying in his bear shape. With a snarl, he felt his claws retract. Felt his body change as he dropped, just managing to snag one times scaly claw. He pulled himself up, grabbing the scaly leg with his other hand. The beast didn't respond to him. It had to know he was there. He risked a glance upward. Golden fur... no, feathers... then again, maybe a mixture of both? It was difficult to see – the wind still stung his eyes, causing them to water.

The human was hanging limp in the other claw. Her hair hung over her face. She looked okay. At least he hoped she was okay. It was hard to tell. She had to be. Gage wished he could call out to her, but he didn't want to do anything that would alert the creature to him. The thing was fucking huge. Could snap him in half without even trying.

He could only pray that he was able to hold on long enough. It wasn't like he had a choice. Gage had to try to find Alice and the cubs. There was also Callum's female. He had also sworn he would protect this female and planned on making good on that promise.

<hr />

Her head hurt too much to open her eyes. It was

throbbing at her temples. Her mouth was seriously dry as well. As in, she had to work to pull it off the roof of her mouth. She finally cracked her eyes open and stared at the ceiling. Edith frowned. It was high and domed, with wooden trusses and what looked like slate tiles.

What?

She tried to recall a ceiling that looked like this and failed. She had never seen this ceiling before. Was she back at the shifter village? *No!* The walls were stone. She winced as she rose to a sitting position. *Good god!* The floor looked like it was made from solid gold. Gleaming, shining, hurt-your-eyes gold. She rubbed them with her knuckles, taking another look. *Yep! Gold.* Maybe even real gold. She arched her back; her neck felt stiff, so Edith rolled her shoulders.

Shit!

It all came back to her. She'd been abducted just like the others. At least, she was pretty sure that was the case, since one second she'd been on Gage's back and the next she'd been shooting up... up... up. Then nothing. She must have blacked out, because her next memory was of waking up here.

She was on a bed. A huge bed. It was covered in furs. As in dead animal skins. There was a stone wall to the one side, closing something off. Had to be a bathroom. It was otherwise completely bare. No, not completely. There was a side table which held a golden goblet and a glass jug of water. She swallowed hard, her tongue feeling too thick. Her mouth sticky.

Edith carefully moved to the side and filled the goblet. She gave the contents a sniff. Maybe it was poisoned. That was stupid. If they wanted her dead, she'd be done for already. That left drugs. What if they wanted her drugged up and pliant? She took a small, tentative sip. Edith groaned softly because the cool liquid felt that amazing going down her throat. The whole drug thing didn't make sense either. Whatever it was that had taken her was big and strong, it certainly didn't need drugs to control her.

Edith downed the glass, feeling sick to her stomach. She put a hand on her belly and took a deep breath. Her mind worked overtime. What did it want with her? They had taken mostly women and a couple of kids. It didn't make any sense. She tried to tamp down the panic that threatened to overtake her.

A breeze caught her hair, which blew gently across her face. There was an opening on the one side of the strange room. No doors, no windows, only the one really large opening, with a kind of stone ledge.

Edith carefully slid off the thick mattress, it was much higher than your run-of-the-mill bed and was much bigger in general than any bed she had ever seen. She carefully stood up, still feeling a little queasy but, thankfully, not in any imminent danger of keeling over or throwing up. Then she walked over to the opening, gripping the wall as she came closer. She felt her eyes widen and even gasped. The sound reverberated around the room.

Edith was in a high tower. Literally a Rapunzel tower. Pity her hair was only shoulder-length or she'd have a means to escape. She held back a hysterical laugh as she looked down over the edge, still holding onto the wall. This was just crazy! There were many such towers and as far as the eye could see. There was no way in or out of the tower. No stairs. No elevators. No rungs. Nothing, just sheer stone walls.

Then she saw it.

Her breath caught. The creature. Or one of them at least. Its great wings flapped as it came closer and closer and closer still. Yep! It was focused on her alright. Her heart beat faster. Her armpits felt instantly clammy.

A griffin?

Yes, it had to be. Yet, it was unlike any picture she'd seen in any of the books her brother used to pour over. Firstly, its beak was more of a gold color. It even glinted in the sun. It was sharp and hooked and deadly looking. Perfect for tearing flesh. *Not thinking about that!* The head of an eagle. Well, not like any eagle she had ever seen. Firstly, it had ears, they were feathered but definitely ears. Then, its feathers were more of a gleaming caramel color. Lighter around the head, becoming darker down its huge, muscular body. There were clearly feathers on its head, neck and wings and fur on the lower body, with a mix in the middle. Its front feet were scaled talons, like an eagle, with the back legs and paws of a lion.

It made a screeching noise. Not a pleasant sound. The noise did make her realize how close it was. Its eyes on her. The cold, pale eyes of a predator. That much was clear. Bright yellow irises seemed to zone in on her. Its great wings flapped slowly and completely noiselessly. It was amazing how light it looked, despite its massive bulk.

Edith swallowed heavily. She carefully retraced her steps backwards, not taking her eyes off of it. Trying to move slowly. No sudden movements! That was a rule, wasn't it? *Don't turn your back.* If need be, make yourself as big as possible, wave your arms and make plenty of noise. That way you could scare away whatever wild creature was after you. It worked sometimes. *Yeah, well, no!* She got the distinct feeling it wouldn't work in this case. The back of her calves hit the bed as the griffin landed on the ledge, its claws scraping on the stone, taking up the entire opening, which up until now had seemed enormous. Moving more quickly, she skirted around the bed, until the hard, stone wall was at her back. There was nowhere else to go. Even though the room was perfectly round, she was cornered.

Now up close – far too close for comfort – she could see that its beak wasn't pure gold. It had a golden color because of thin threads or veins that ran through it. The scales on its front legs were also golden-tinged. Its tail. *Oh boy, it had a tail.* A tail that almost reached the top of the high, dome-like roof. It was long and feline. Only, instead of a fur tuft on the end, there were a couple of those caramel colored feathers. He swished his tail a few times before she heard that familiar cracking noise.

She pulled in a sharp breath as she watched the griffin collapse into itself. Folding back one muscle, one sinew at a time until a tall, hulking beast of a man stood before her.

A man.

No, not a man. Not even close. "You're a griffin shifter," she whispered.

"Griffin?" He frowned, cocking his head. His lips were full, his nose wide. He looked like he ate steroids for breakfast and testosterone for lunch with maybe a side of human for dinner. He was naked – enormous, everywhere. She kept her eyes on his, not wanting to give him any ideas. The weirdest thing about him, aside from his sheer size, was that he still had yellow-tinged irises, just like an eagle. His eyes were big and strangely beautiful. His hair was overgrown, it hung about his shoulders like a shining, shaggy, black mane.

"What is this 'griffin'?" His voice was smooth like honey, it had a methodic ring to it. He could speak.

Thank god!

Not only that, she could understand him, which meant that he would be able to understand her too. *Oh good! Shew!* This way, he would know what she was saying when she was begging for mercy or negotiating for her freedom. Possibly both at the same time.

Oh flip! He'd asked her a question. "You," she blurted. "You're a griffin shifter. Aren't you?"

His frown deepened, and he shook his head. "I am one of The Feral."

The Feral.

'The'?

Why not just feral? Because, um, yep, he sure was. She narrowed her eyes. "What do you want with me?" The million-dollar question.

He cocked his head in the other direction. It looked like he was scrutinizing her. Not good! Her heart leapt to her throat as he began to walk towards her. "Stop right there." Edith put her hand up.

He stopped but only for a moment before closing the distance between them. She had to crane her neck to maintain eye contact. His gaze drifted over her body. It seemed both thorough and clinical. At least, she hoped he wasn't checking her out in any way. His nostrils flared a couple of times. "What?" She resisted the urge to fold her arms across her chest.

He pushed out a breath. Moving quicker than she thought possible, he reached around her and gripped her ass in both his hands.

"No! What?" She gripped his forearms. Flipping hell but they were thick and muscular, just like the rest of him. She tried to pry him off her. "Stop that!" she yelled.

The shifter... guy... griffin shifter ignored her efforts and squeezed her ass. Squeezed. Her. Ass. *The nerve!* He made a rumbling noise. Then he was letting her ass go but only so that he could grope her boobs. *What the hell!* Another rumble.

This was too much. Too damned much. She slapped him a shot. Pain shot up her arm and two of her nails broke. Two. The good news was that he let her go and even took a step back. The shifter nodded once. "Leukos the Great will like you."

Edith licked her lips; she hated the sound of that. "Who is Leukos?"

"King of all," the shifter announced. "Come." He picked her up and held her against him with just one arm.

"No! Stop!" she yelled. "Put me down." She pushed at his chest. Then she realized that he was headed for the opening. *Oh shit!* This wasn't good. "Hey! Stop!" She fought harder, kicking him. Doing everything short of hurting herself to get him to let her go.

The griffin – whatever he was – launched himself off the ledge. Freefalling. It wasn't fun. The ground rushing up to meet you. The feeling of weightlessness. All of it. Not fun at all, terrifying was a better description, especially since she didn't have a parachute or a backup plan. Edith screamed bloody murder. It took her a good couple of seconds before she comprehended that she was no longer about to die but safely – relatively speaking – in his firm grip. His talons were wrapped around her middle. By this time, her throat felt raw from screaming. The terror did not abate though. She had a feeling she wasn't going to like meeting this Leukos person. Why did her ass and her breasts make any difference to whether he liked her or not? *Oh god!* She didn't want to even think of the answer to that question.

CHAPTER 7

G age paced backwards and forwards. Up and down. On and on. It wasn't very practical, but it did help him to stay calm. Relatively calm considering his heart was racing and that adrenaline pumped. He could scent it on himself.

His left eye was still swollen shut. His skull felt like it might be fractured. The minor abrasions had since healed. The rest would too, and in no time.

Shifters. These fuckers were shifters. The... what was it Edith had called the creature... something mythological? He couldn't recall. He hadn't given her theory much mind at the time. A lion-eagle with magical powers. He still wanted to snort. It sounded absurd, too crazy to contemplate. Still did, even though he knew it to be true. At least the lion-eagle part was true.

Fuck.

There was no way out of this room. Nowhere to go but down. To jump to his freedom. He would die from the impact, that was almost a foregone conclusion. However, he would also regenerate and come back. Would someone notice his bloody corpse before he had a chance to sufficiently heal? Very likely. Even if he did manage to get away with it, he couldn't leave without the female. Without the others as well. Frustration ate at him. Gage grit his teeth.

Where in hell was he? If he left with the intention of bringing others back with him, would he even find the place again? If he did, and he returned with every shifter, would they be able to stand against this formidable enemy? He allowed his eyes to roam over the vast plain and counted hundreds of such towers. How many of these things were there? Too fucking many.

The creature that had knocked him unconscious hadn't so much as uttered a word. They'd arrived at this place – here in the middle of no-fucking-where – and the beast had lowered itself to just above the ground. Gage hadn't stood a chance; one hard shake of the talon and he was on the ground. At least he managed to land on his feet. So much for being a big lumbering bear. Not that it mattered much, because one more swipe of that same talon had knocked him the fuck out. He'd woken up here a half an hour ago. Good to know that it had chosen to let him live. So far, it was the only thing he had going for him. Why though? These creatures didn't want him there. Why not simply finish him?

A loud screech drew him back to the large doorway. If that's what it could be called. The opening served as both door and window. He leaned out, scouting the perimeter. One of them was flying towards a tower to the left of him. It drew closer and closer. He couldn't see the doorway of that tower from this angle. It disappeared into the tower. These large spaces were obviously being used as dwellings. They had to be. He looked around the sparse room for what felt like the hundredth time.

The bed was covered in furs. If only he had a knife – something to cut them into long strips. He'd be able to fashion a rope and escape. Same problem though – how would he make it back up the tower with the human? Which of the hundreds of towers housed Alice, Edith and the others? He doubted he'd be able to scent them from all the way on the ground. Frustration ate at him. What the fuck was he going to do next? How long until they decided to kill him? Then he'd be of no use at all.

More of the creatures flew by, making their way to various towers.

His hackles went up. Gage had heard something that sounded like a scream. Not only that, it had sounded distinctly female. He held his breath. "Stop it!" It was the human. The sound was muted. He was sure she was yelling otherwise he wouldn't have heard her.

There was more shouting. Something that sounded like, "No! Stop!" and then, a garbled sentence he couldn't make out, followed by, "Hey! Stop!"

Adrenaline coursed through him and he leapt onto the ledge, craning his head. It was coming from the tower that beast had just entered. There was a godawful scream that he felt deep in his core. Just as Gage was about to launch himself off the edge – broken bones be damned – he saw it. It was the creature as it flew from the tower. The beast had the female clasped tightly in his talons, quickly moving away.

Edith sucked in a deep breath and screamed again, this time it sounded more angry than fearful. Where the fuck was it taking her? *Fuck this!*

Gage roared. It didn't help their situation any, but it made him feel marginally better. He sucked in a deep breath and slowly released it. It was time for action. No more sitting around and twiddling his damned thumbs.

It was hard work to hold a partial shift but that was too damned bad because he needed to do this and right now. His nails lengthened and thickened some, as did his jaw. Fur had sprouted in tufts on his body, it was especially prevalent on his arms and legs. His nails were thick and clumsy. Right now, panther claws would have been fantastic. He'd use what he had, which was better than nothing. Gage sat down on the bed and began to slowly tear strips off of the fur hides. It was slow, tedious work. He was forced to take frequent breaks, changing back into his human shape. He compelled himself to keep at it and, in the end, was very glad he had.

The asshole griffin carried her up and around all of the towers, they passed a couple more of the creatures. The big beasts would hover on the spot. One or two of them would come in closer and sniff so loud she could hear it. Other than that, they were eerily silent. Even the flapping of their great wings was noiseless.

She noticed that there were subtle differences in each of their plumage – for lack of a better word. Some were a deeper chocolate caramel. Some were more of a golden color. There were a couple of darker ones as well. Their beaks and scales were also varying degrees of gold.

Oh!

It looked like they were making their way to a tower in the distance. It was perched on a hilly outcrop and looked to be bigger than the ones they had left behind them. As they flew higher up the outcrop, she noticed that the ocean lay on the other side. The water was framed by wide expanses of beaches, but not like any beaches she had ever seen. These had pebbles instead of sand.

There was no time to appreciate the view because the distance to the tower was diminishing fast. Edith felt her stomach lurch. It was probably the fact that they were flying a good two or three floors from the ground, or the claw that clasped her firmly around her waist. The talons on this creature were ridiculous.

Her heart beat faster as they reached the opening. The griffin stood on the ledge with his back legs and put her down.

The space was so much bigger than the first tower, at least four, possibly even five times bigger. There was a man in the room. Another one of the griffin shifters. She could tell by his eyes. He had the same predatory gaze. A gaze that focused with shocking intensity and missed nothing. His irises were more golden than fiery yellow.

There were cracking noises behind her, but she didn't take her eyes off of the guy in front of her.

This griffin was slightly bigger, he wore a loincloth. She wasn't going to complain about his choice of clothing though because she was just infinitely glad that his junk was covered. The cloth looked like it had been made from soft leather. His thighs were well-muscled, like the rest of him. It was definitely a shifter thing. These guys more so than the regular shifters. In her opinion, they were too damned big. Far too imposing. The guy smiled – or tried to. He thankfully gave up. Probably when he caught the look of horror on her face.

She hugged herself. Thankful that Gage had made her dress more appropriately for the trip. She wished she was wearing more. Especially when his eyes moved down the length of her and then back, lingering on her breasts before lifting to meet her eyes.

"Come in." He gestured for her to move closer. His voice had that same rich melodic quality. His hair was much lighter. Honey blond if she were to take a guess. There was a girl in her first year at college who liked to say her hair was honey blond. Not simply blond but honey blond. His was the same shade. Not that it mattered. Not right now. Nothing mattered other than talking some sense into these Neanderthals.

"Come in," he repeated.

Not hardly. She stayed right where she was. "I want to go home." She decided to make her position clear from the get-go.

"No." He shook his head, not looking as happy as before. "You will stay."

Okie dokie. This was going well. Not. "Um... I don't want to stay. You can't keep me here against my will."

"I can." He folded his arms and tilted his chin slightly upward.

That was it. No explanation. No discussion. Just boom, you're staying.

"Why am I even here? What do you want with me?" She shouldn't have asked, and yet she needed to know. It would be better if she knew what the hell was going on even if she hated his response. She wasn't a pessimist by nature, but she got the distinct feeling that she was going to hate it.

"I am a keythong."

When she realized that nothing more was forthcoming, she asked, "A what?" She sighed in exasperation, feeling irritation well in her. "It would be really great if you could speak English. It would help things enormously. What do you want with me?" She enunciated every word of the question.

The big griffin pushed out a heavy breath, he looked over her shoulder at the guy behind her. "These beings are spirited."

"Yes, they are," he responded. It sounded like he was smiling.

"I am still not convinced that we would be compatible with them." The big guy cocked his head to the other side and gave her the once-over all over again, looking thoughtful. He was definitely sizing her up, which she didn't like.

There was only one thing that made her feel slightly better and that was how indifferent he remained. He lifted his head and sniffed the air. Then he walked over to her. Edith couldn't go backwards because the other guy was there, so she stood her ground.

He dropped to his knees in front of her and sniffed again.

She wanted to give him a kick to the face but that probably wasn't a good idea. "Stop that." What a jerk!

He got back up and even took a step or two back. Edith could breathe a little easier. Then he nodded once. "Unmated." He shrugged. "That is at least something. This one is a bit bigger than the other one. Maybe she will withstand a mounting."

Say what? *Oh shit! No! Hell no!* This was what she had

UNCHAINED

been afraid of. Her first thought was to back away, to run, but neither of those were a possibility, so she put her hands on her hips instead.

Do not show fear. Ever.

"Look! I'm not interested. No." She shook her head. "Do you understand that?"

"Of course, I understand," he snorted. "I am Leukos the Great." He puffed out his chest. It was a good chest. He wasn't a bad-looking guy, if you liked seriously rough around the edges, but he wasn't her type. Not even close. Even if he was, it would still be a resounding hell no. The whole kidnapping thing had put a damper on that.

"Good!" she said the word with conviction. "Then you will understand me when I say that I'm not in the least bit interested. You are wasting your time. I would like to go home now. My friends too. You can't keep us here against our will."

"I think it may be you who lacks language skills. I already said no. You are an unattached female. You will stay. One of us will mate you and get you with clutch."

Her mouth fell open for a second. "Firstly," she pointed a finger at him, "I'm not mating anyone. No one is mounting me either. You can forget that." She felt her lungs seize at the thought. If he, or any of the others, wanted to rape her, she wouldn't stand a chance. She forced the thought out of her head. Panicking right now was not going to help her. "Lastly, what the hell is a clutch?" Best to change the subject. Move away from talk of mating and mounting.

"A clutch." He looked at her like she was going mad. "Eggs, young. You know what an egg is don't you?"

"Of course I know what an egg is, I just don't know what an egg has to do with me?"

"I'm not sure about these beings," he addressed the other one again, looking back over her shoulder. "They seem dimwitted."

"That may be so, but they are well suited to our needs. If they can mate and produce with the wolf and bear males, then they can do so with us too." He sounded so nonchalant as he doled out her fate. "There is only one way to find out."

"Please stop talking about me as if I'm not in the room," Edith piped up. "I'm not dimwitted. I just don't understand what an egg has to do with anything."

Leukos the Great – she gave a mental eye roll at his name – took a step forward as he began talking. "One of us will mount you to test that it is possible – I have my doubts – and then you will be mated. Do you understand so far or – ?"

"No one touches me. Not so much as a finger." She tried to sound tough.

"Did you check this one for compatibility?" Leukos ignored her flat.

"My name is Edith. Please don't call me 'being' or 'this one' or whatever other name you have in mind." She should probably tone it down a touch since she was on the back foot here. It wasn't in her nature, so she ignored the little voice telling her to tread carefully.

"No, I didn't even try to undress her. I could tell that she would fight me like the other one did."

"Meredith is just as lively." Leukos widened his eyes like it was all giving him a headache. *Well tough luck, buddy!*

Meredith.

She was the other woman who had been taken. "Is Meredith alright? Have you harmed her?" Edith tried to keep from yelling at him.

"Of course, she's in good health," Leukos snorted again. He gave her a questioning look. Like he thought she was a nut job. "We're not barbaric. It has been established that I am too large for her, so I instructed that my warriors find me another potential mate."

Too large.

Oh brother! This was not happening. Please let this not be happening. She shuddered. "Not me." She shook her head. "I'm not your girl."

"This one," the guy behind her cleared his throat, "Edith is sturdier. Much better suited, Great One. Wider hips, bigger chest. I am sure her female organ will be bigger too."

"I cannot believe what I am hearing." Edith felt like sticking her fingers in her ears and making loud noises. "What you are referring to is rape... forced sex," she added when Leukos frowned, looking confused.

"Leave us, Soren. I want to become acquainted with our guest."

She shook her head, looking back. The other shifter was turning to leave. "Soren," she shouted his name and he turned back. "Don't go. I'm not interested in becoming acquainted with him, you or any of you."

"I am not giving you a choice in the matter," Leukos said before turning to Soren. "Now go." His gentle, melodious voice turned steely.

"Wait!" she shouted, but Soren was already shifting and leaping from the window.

"We are a good people." Leukos looked at her with such sincerity. "I am a good keythong and not just any keythong but the…"

"Yeah, yeah… Leukos the Great."

He nodded, a glint evident in his eyes. "Yes, I am king of all. I am not familiar with the way of your beings, or," he sighed, "with females in general but I will do my very best to please you."

"You're really starting to piss me off. I'm not sure how to convey this without losing my cool. I'm not interested."

"I am strong, powerful. I'm ruler of all." He shrugged. "I have untold riches." He pointed around the room. At the golden chandelier. At the gleaming gold floors, at the ornate golden doorframe. Not that the opening was a door exactly but what did it matter when she was about to be raped.

"I can make you very happy." He looked at her earnestly. "Tell me how to please you and I will do it." His yellow eyes seemed to brighten.

At least he was trying to convince her before he jumped her. "Thank you for the kind offer but I'm not interested. I don't know you."

"I told you, I'm Leukos the—"

"That's your name, it's not who you are. I would need time to get to know you and to…" *Oh shit! Mistake. Big mistake.* Her and her big mouth. "I don't mean it like…"

He smiled. Feral was the right description. Their name suited them big time. "That is no problem. We have all the time in the world to get to know one another. We can spend every waking hour together and you will warm my furs at night."

"No! I don't want to warm your furs. I'm sure you're a great guy but I'm not interested." For whatever reason, her mind wandered back to Gage. To her instant attraction to him. It was either something you felt for someone or something you didn't.

"Given time—"

She shook her head. "I know that it will never happen. It's not that there's something wrong with you or anything. You're a good-looking guy... keythong." She hoped keythong was the right word. "Very good-looking but you're just not my type."

The huge, very buff king of the griffins sighed heavily and sank down on a nearby chair. "I don't understand it." He shook his head, looking distraught. "The Feral are a strong species. The strongest of all the species, and yet not one female has shown even the slightest interest in mating with us. Not one would allow any of the males to mount her."

Was this guy for real? "You can't go around kidnapping women and then expect them to allow you to have sex with them. That's not how it works. You clearly have zero understanding of our species. I'm not sure how things work out here, but that is not how it happens in my world."

"But keythongs and females are meant to be together. To mate and have young." He shrugged. "That is the point isn't it?"

"No, that is the result." She didn't think she was getting through to him. "Love is the point and having children is the result. Two people need to meet in a natural way. In a natural setting. They need to hit it off."

"Hit it off? What would they hit, surely not one

another? You are very strange beings." He shook his head.

Edith had to chew on her lower lip to stop herself from laughing. Was this guy serious? "I don't mean literally hit as in... never mind. What I meant was that they need to get along and be attracted to each other." He still looked somewhat confused. "They need to be compatible." She used his word in the end.

"Ah, I understand. What you are saying is that the mounting should be enjoyable." His eyes glinted and he smiled.

"No... yes, but no, that's not entirely correct." She paused gathering her thoughts. "They should want to have sex... mount, but that is not the most important part of it. They should like each other and talk. They should spend time together. Do fun things not involving sex. It should not be forced in any way. Given time, they would become physical and expand their relationship. They might move in together. Live together and then yes, they would eventually marry... mate with each other and start a family. It takes time and two willing people. How do you guys go about things? Your womenfolk can't be too impressed with your abducting of human women. Why would you want to replace them like that?"

He clenched his jaw, his eyes clouded. "There are only twelve remaining females."

"Remaining?" Her voice was laced with shock. "What happened to them all?"

His Adam's apple bobbed as he swallowed. "They all died from the clutch sickness."

"There's that word again. It's familiar but I can't place it. What is a clutch?"

"Our females do not give birth to live young, like the shifters and you humans. You do give birth to live young, do you not?" His brows raised, and he seemed to look at her for acknowledgment.

"Yes." She nodded. "That is correct."

"It is what we observed." He shifted in the chair. "The Feral are part eagle. Not your normal run-of-the-mill eagle." He made a face like the thought was obscene. "We are related to the now extinct phoenix. It's a distant relation but still a relation nonetheless."

She nodded, taking a seat on the edge of the bed.

"Our females give birth," he sucked in a deep breath, "give birth to a clutch of eggs, normally two or three."

"Oh, okay." She nodded a bit too vigorously because hey, eggs. Come on! She was entitled to feeling a little shell-shocked. *Shell!* She stifled a giggle. This was all too much, and she was clearly losing her ever-loving mind.

"One after one, they all died," he said. "We could find no cure. There was nothing we could do."

"Stop having eggs."

He shook his head. "We are born to procreate. To continue the species. We are driven to do so. The drive is almost beyond our control. Even though we all knew, including our females, that they would most likely die, they still chose to try."

"Wow! That's awful." She couldn't imagine. All of those griffin women, all becoming pregnant and then dying from a sickness."

"It took years. Eight years and ten months to be exact, until every fertile female was gone, barring one. Valintina has chosen to be alone, she lives a life of solitude. That was years ago already. Our males have been without females for far too long."

She could tell. "And the twelve who are left? How is it that they survived?"

"Nine of the females are elders, they can no longer bear a clutch. The other two are barren. The twelfth is Valintina."

"So, the future of your kind is at stake here." It was starting to make sense.

"Yes." He nodded. "That is why we require willing females to take as mates. We need young." His voice had once again become hard and steely. This time with determination. It shone in his amber-colored eyes.

"You do realize that you're going about this the wrong way though, don't you?"

"No. You are here. It is only a matter of time before you choose a male. There are many of us. I am hoping that you decide I am the right—"

"Stop right there." She slumped her shoulders. Frustration ate at her. He hadn't listened to a thing she had said. "I'm not going to agree. Not ever. It's not going to happen. Kidnapping women is not the way to go about this."

"What else should we do? There is no other way."

"You will have to find another way. I don't know. Figure something out. For a start, you need to understand humans better. Our ways, our culture. Here's an idea, get Netflix. Study the programs." She smiled at her own stupid joke.

"What is Netflix?"

"It's television. A box that you watch…" She could see he had no idea. "Never mind that. Observe human women but not in a creepy way."

"Not in a creepy way." He sounded like he was thinking it through.

"Don't spy on them. Spend time with them on their own turf, on their own terms. For a start, you can't walk around naked. It's not how we do things."

Leukos looked down.

"Yeah, no, I'm afraid a piece of leather ain't going to cut it. You need jeans and a t-shirt. You need actual human clothing." Just then, her stomach grumbled. It had been forever since she had last eaten.

His head cocked to the side and his gaze moved to her belly.

"I'm sorry, I'm hungry. What do you guys eat? I'm sure it's a lot."

"Oh, how rude of me. You must go and take nourishment. I'll have Soren bring you back once you have finished."

She faked a big yawn. "Actually, I'm also really exhausted. It's been a long day." Truth was, she didn't want to come back. Not ever! "Unless of course Soren wants to take me home." Edith thought she'd try her luck.

"No!" Leukos's eyes narrowed. "You have much to explain. It seems we have a lot to learn about humans if we are to mate them."

"Okay, fine. I'll answer some more of your questions and help you out by giving some information, but then I'm done and you let me go." A win-win situation if she ever heard one. Edith held her breath.

Leukos, the great dickhead, shook his head, infuriating her. "We will talk but you are not leaving. You will stay. You will make a good mate."

Edith rolled her eyes preparing to argue.

"It's no use, you will not be able to change my mind." Then he rose to his feet. She watched as he walked to the opening. She quickly looked away when she realized his ass was bare. They really had to work on their dressing skills. They had a ton of things they needed to work on.

Leukos made a high-pitched whistling noise. It had that same melodic quality as his voice. There was an answering screech as her lift arrived. She had a feeling that the coming period was going to be taxing on her patience. It didn't seem like he was going to force himself on her. Right now, at least. Then again, words from their conversation came back to her. It sounded like they had checked Meredith out, finding her too small in ways she didn't want to think of. How had they checked to find this out? By trying to rape her? She would be next. Edith chewed on her lower lip. She definitely wasn't out of the woods yet. Worry churned in her gut.

CHAPTER 8

*I*t was show time.

Gage gave the area a final check. All was quiet and had been for some time. That male who had brought him there earlier had returned with food. The male had refused to answer any questions. He'd essentially tossed a basket into the room and headed back out. Jumping from the ledge before Gage could get a paw on him. These beasts weren't interested in him. That much was clear. Gage had forced himself to eat it all, even though his stomach was tied in serious knots. Meat, charred on the outside, still raw on the inside. A flatbread and some berries.

He'd breathed a sigh of relief when the same male had brought Edith back some hours ago. She had seemed unharmed. There was no more screaming. He hoped she was okay. The male had brought her food as well.

Gage gazed from the window, it was dark out, except for a few of the towers that still had fires or candles lit.

He could tell by the way the light danced at the openings. None of those fuckers had ventured out since dusk had fallen two hours ago. There was a part of him that knew he should probably wait until everyone was asleep, but they needed all the time they could get if they wanted to escape. Gage had a feeling these beasts would be after them the moment they knew the two of them were missing. He only hoped it would be morning before that happened.

Gage tested his leather rope one more time, giving it a hard yank. He'd tied it to the torch to the right of the window. It was made from solid gold and seemed sturdy enough. Next, he eased himself over the edge and walked down, slowly easing down the makeshift rope. Gage carefully climbed all the way down. He needed to be sure that its entire length was strong enough. That each and every knot would hold. It seemed that he'd done a good job.

All of his senses firing, he quickly climbed back up, using the rope to assist him. Gage clambered over the edge. It felt good to have solid footing again. Moving quickly, he pulled the whole length back up, rolling it around his arm in a wide circle. Then he untied it from the torch. Gage tied the shorter piece he had left on the bed around his waist. He hauled the looped rope over his shoulder.

On high alert, he reassessed that the perimeter was still clear and lowered himself over the rim. Now, he would have to tread very carefully. Painstakingly so, because dying was not fun. Regenerating was even worse. Hours of agony. Not fun at all!

The tower had been built from stones. It wasn't much, but there was a bit of an edge on each rough rock to hold onto. Gage partially shifted so that he could use his nails as well, wishing for the second time today that he had been born as a panther or a wolf instead of a bear. Curved, sharp nails would have worked so much better than long, thick ones. He would have to suck it up and make do.

Going much slower, he made his way down, one hand-hold and one foot-hold at a time. It was slow going. He was covered in a light sheen of sweat by the time he made it to the bottom. Gage shifted back into his human form and went down onto his haunches for a few minutes so that he could catch his breath. It was still completely quiet, except for the sound of his breathing. One or two more candles had been snuffed. It seemed that these creatures didn't move around much at night.

Good!

Gage rose silently to his feet and made his way to the tower where the human was being held. After partially shifting, he began to climb. It was just as slow. He lost his footing more than once. By the time he made it to the ledge, his arms were shaking and sweat dripped off of him. He quickly pulled himself into the room and removed the ropes, placing them by the opening. Ready for their escape.

Edith was fast asleep. Curled up in a ball under one of the larger furs. He touched the side of her arm, quickly sealing a hand over her mouth when she tried to scream. Her eyes were wide. Her chest rose and fell as she sucked air through her nose.

"It's me," he whispered.

It took a few seconds for his words to register. Her eyes went from wide and fearful to reflecting pure relief.

She huffed out a breath as he removed his hand. "Gage?"

"Shhhh. Yes," he smiled, "it's me." He'd never been so happy to see someone. She looked fine. He couldn't scent those males on her.

She made a sobbing noise and launched herself at him, her arms going around his neck. He instinctively folded his arms around her.

He realized with a start that she was crying softly.

"I promised I would keep you safe and I meant it." He stroked the hair at the back of her head. It was soft.

She tensed slightly in his arms.

"You okay?" he whispered.

"You're naked, aren't you?"

"Yep… I'm afraid so."

"I hate to tell you, but you're also really hot and sweaty."

He couldn't help but notice that she didn't pull away. "Climbing up and down stone walls will do that to a male."

She let him go. "I've never been so afraid in my whole life."

"I'm here now. We need to move though."

Her eyes widened. "Move how? Where?"

"We're getting out of here. Tonight… right now."

She swallowed thickly. "You don't mean…? Look, unless you magically sprouted wings, I don't think—"

"I made a leather rope. I'll tie you to my back. The longer rope is over there." He pointed to where it lay. "I'll use it to slowly lower us down…" He stopped there because she was shaking her head really hard.

"That's dangerous!" She sucked in a deep breath.

"What if…"

"I'm strong."

"What if the rope snaps?" Her breathing quickened.

It was Gage's turn to swallow thickly.

"You're not entirely sure this will work, are you?" Even though she was still whispering, her voice had grown high-pitched.

"It's not without risk. If we fall, I will be sure to take the brunt of the impact. We will move quickly and carefully." He shook his head. "The only other option is to leave you here while I—"

"No!"

"Shhhhh." He put a finger to his lips. "We can't alert them. We have to leave soon. It's up to you. I don't want to leave you here. I'm pretty sure I can get us down in one piece."

"I'm afraid. Afraid to stay but afraid to climb down the side of a sheer wall too." Her eyes were wide and filled with definite fear. Before he could say anything more, she pulled back her shoulders. "I can't stay here. These guys, they—"

Anger gnawed at him. "You can tell me all about it later. I take it you're coming?"

Edith chewed on her lower lip for a second or two before nodding once.

"You don't look sure." It looked like Gage was raising his brows. It was hard to see much in the dark. Especially considering it was a half moon. At least the stars were pretty bright.

"I'm not sure at all, but it doesn't mean I'm staying."

This was the most stupid thing she had ever agreed to. Her gut churned and her whole body felt clammy all of a sudden.

She looked around for her shoes and put them on, tying the laces.

"You need to be very quiet."

She nodded. "Understood. We don't have any food or water or—"

"Don't worry about any of that. I'm quite capable of looking after us."

Of that she had no doubt. "How did you get here?"

"I grabbed onto the beast that took you and hung on for the ride. You were out cold."

"That sounds really dangerous." She widened her eyes. "What if you had fallen?"

"I gave you my word I would protect you and I meant it."

"Thank you!" She reached out and touched the side of his arm. At least she hoped it was his arm.

Gage shifted his weight on the bed. "Maybe tie one of those smaller furs around your shoulders." He lifted his arm.

She felt around until she found one that didn't weigh a ton and tied the arms around herself.

Gage was busy by the opening; it looked like – from what little she could see – he was tying the one end of the long rope onto the golden torch. She watched his large silhouette as he leaned out, scanning the area before turning around. It was too dark to see much otherwise, thankfully, considering he was butt naked.

Gage walked back to where she was standing and

lowered himself, bending at the knee. "Climb aboard," he whispered.

She gripped his shoulders and did as he said, trying hard to avoid his man-part. Maybe it was good she couldn't see much. Her eyeballs were going to need a serious wash after this.

He walked backwards, lowering them onto the bed. "Tie this around your waist, make it snug and use a double knot."

Again, she complied. Gage gave the twine rope a sharp tug, checking to see if she had done a decent job. Then he tied the other end of the rope around himself, giving the twine another sharp tug. "Ready?" he asked.

"I guess." Her voice was a bit shaky. Was she really going to do this?

He gripped her thighs and rose to a standing position. "Um, you're going to need to lock your feet around my waist." She could hear that he was smiling.

"Okay." She really didn't want to be anywhere near… that part of him.

"Watch out for…"

For his *you-know-what*. "Yeah, I will," she quickly replied, locking her feet as he had instructed. His abs felt rock hard, as did the rest of him.

"I've got this," he whispered, his voice deep and assuring.

"I know."

"You're shaking."

"Do you blame me?" *Oh god! Oh god!* She tried not to grip him too tightly. Tried not to think about what was about to happen. Despite not knowing him, she trusted

Gage. He had somehow managed to track her down. He hadn't given up, and now was about to rescue her.

"I guess I can't blame you for being afraid. We'll be okay. Let's do this." Was he trying to convince himself or her?

"Okay." Her voice hitched.

Gage stood on the edge; he gave the rope that would be their lifeline a hard yank before lowering them out in the open. His muscles bunched and hardened. Edith whimpered, having to hold on tight as gravity pulled her down. She squeezed her eyes shut. She wasn't sure she could hold on until they got to the bottom. If she fell, would the makeshift rope hold? Would she end up pulling Gage down with her?

Gage paused for the longest time, not doing anything. They just hung out several floors from the ground. It was getting more and more difficult to hold on. What was wrong? Why had he stopped? She was about to ask when he pulled them back onto the ledge, stepping back into the room. "What is it?" she whispered, her voice quivered.

"We're doing this the wrong way. I need you tied to my chest. You might end up slipping and dragging us down. Also," his body tensed, "if we fall – though I'm sure we won't – as a precaution, I want you on top so that I'll definitely land first."

"Oh, so you like it when the lady is on top." She gave a whispered snicker. *Why had she said that?* She really needed to get a handle on these nerves. "Okay. That's fine," she quickly said, trying to cover up for her bad joke. "I think it's a better idea that I'm on top," she added, wishing she could stick her foot in her mouth to shut herself up.

Gage ignored her stupid statements. He walked back to the bed and they went through the motions of untying the rope. It wasn't easy after securing the thing so tightly in the first place. She climbed off the bed.

There was a soft patting noise which she realized was him tapping his thighs with his hands. "You need to straddle my lap. I'm sorry I…"

"It's fine. I get it. We don't have much choice here." Her cheeks burned. She hoped he couldn't see her but by the way he moved around the room, she got the feeling his eyesight was pretty darned perfect.

"You don't have to feel embarrassed about this. It's not a big deal." He could obviously sense her apprehension and was trying to make her feel better. It was really sweet.

Although his words had helped, they didn't eradicate the tension. "I can't help it. I apologize upfront if, you know," she had to stop herself from giggling, "I touch you… you know." She closed her eyes, feeling like a total idiot. It was a distinct possibility, given how they would be tied to one another and given that he was bare-ass naked. *Why was this such a big deal?* He was trying to help her. This wasn't sexual in any way.

"It is what it is. Just as long…" He pulled in a breath though his nose, slowly releasing it. "Just as long as you understand if I accidentally react in any way. Given the circumstances, I'm sure it won't be the case, but…" He scratched the back of his head, clearly also a little embarrassed by this whole thing. She found it sweeter than sweet. It was turning out that Gage wasn't the asshole she thought he was.

"Sure thing," she blurted. "No worries." Although she meant every word, for a moment, she was tempted to stay. Who could blame her? Edith didn't want to die or get seriously hurt. It was also the embarrassment of the whole thing, but she'd rather be tied to a very naked Gage than face Leukos and his crew in the morning.

The Feral.

She shivered.

"Good." She heard that patting sound again. "Climb aboard."

"Oh, right." She stood on the bed and then threw a leg over him, carefully lowering herself until sitting on his thighs. As far away from *there* as she could get.

Gage gripped her hips and apologized. She was about to tell him he didn't have to keep saying he was sorry when he pulled her flush again him and there it was. Right there at her core. His *you-know-what.* He was a big guy, of course she knew it because she had seen for herself, but right now she could feel it. Not that he was hard in any way. Just big. She had to stop thinking like this. Her cheeks felt like they were on fire. Gage lifted her so that things weren't quite as intimate. "You okay?"

She made a sound of agreement, not quite trusting her voice.

"Good. Let's get this rope tied," he whispered. "I don't want to take any chances." He reached around her and tied the rope around her first before securing her to himself. Gage stood up, walking back to the opening. He leaned in a little. "Hold on tight."

"Okay." She wrapped her arms around his neck and locked her feet at her ankles, which were at his back.

"Trust me." It wasn't a question but a statement. "Still

and quiet."

She nodded. Her cheek brushed against the stubble of his.

"Good," a soft vibration.

His whole body tightened as he lowered them off of the ledge. They were almost parallel to the ground. Edith made the mistake of looking down. *Holy crap!* She grabbed him tighter.

"Easy," Gage whispered. "I've got you."

She pushed out a deep breath before pulling in another one. Edith closed her eyes. *Not looking!* It wasn't nearly as dark outside as it had been indoors. She had been able to see the ground and – more importantly – the fact that it was far away. If they fell… no, she couldn't think like that.

She stifled a yell when they started to move. They were going more quickly than she expected. It would be over soon. *Please let it be over soon. Please let them make it. Oh god!*

Down, down, down. Her stomach was tied in knots. It lurched as they dropped a little faster. She swallowed hard and sucked in a deep breath. The last thing she wanted was to throw up, especially considering chances were good that Gage would become collateral damage.

They continued their descent. It couldn't be far now. Surely? She was too afraid to open her eyes.

There was a sudden hard jerk. Gage growled as they began to freefall. The drop lasted all of two seconds. She groaned as her back hit the stone wall. Hard enough to bruise but not so hard as to cause any type of long-term damage.

Gage was breathing hard, one of his arms was raised

above his head and the other clutched a rock to the left of them. "Shhhh," he whispered straight into her ear. So soft, she could barely hear him. She clutched his shoulders with her hands. Her back still throbbed, the pain becoming more manageable.

There was a rustling noise. It came from the closest tower to them. A silhouette appeared in the opening. Oh no! They were about to be busted. The griffin shifter seemed to lean out of his tower. He didn't shift or sound the alarm though, he just stood there.

What the…?

There was a pushing against her… well, *there…* against her vagina. Gage was flush against her, his breath soft against the top of her head. She'd slipped down during the fall. *Oh good god!* He was becoming erect. Here and now, despite them dangling off the side of a sheer wall, still a good fifteen feet above the ground. Gage had warned her that it could happen, but she didn't think it actually would. Never in a million years. They stayed perfectly still, perfectly quiet. *Go away!* She silently pleaded, keeping her eyes on the griffin, still standing in the opening.

At the same time, she couldn't help but notice that Gage's chest pressed against her own, squashing her breasts. His member pushed against her most sensitive place. Long, thick, hard and oh… oh good god, it was throbbing. Her breath caught in her throat. *Act normal!* Okay, that was pushing it under these circumstances. *Stay calm! Don't react. Oops, too late.*

Her mind may have made a decision, but her body chose to ignore it. Oh boy did it ever! Her girl parts hadn't gotten the 'do not react' memo from her brain.

It was so wrong that her nipples pebbled, that her breath became quicker. That her core began to feel that much more sensitive as he throbbed against her. A groan lodged itself deep in her throat. She succeeded in holding that back, but only just.

The griffin finally moved away. *Thank god!* Using his free hand, Gage gripped her thigh, anchoring her more firmly in place. "Shhhh," he warned as he brushed more firmly against her. It wasn't like this was on purpose or anything. If he moved back, even slightly, she might fall. This was torture. If he let her go, she might slip. Might cry out. They might get caught. They had to be totally quiet. They hung like that for long minutes. The throbbing didn't abate. If anything, it became more insistent. A need slowly began to grow in her. The need to move. Not away. Oh no! It was the need to rub herself against him. It was merely the adrenaline talking. The sheer intensity of this whole situation. That and the feeling of being alive. They weren't far from the ground. The griffin hadn't seen them, but they weren't home free. Not yet.

Throb. Throb.

She heard Gage swallow hard. Could hear him trying to control his erratic breathing. Did he feel it too? Of course he did! He was hard. Her cheeks burned. Her whole body burned with both need and embarrassment. Gage was breathing fast, probably from the exertion of holding them up for so long with only one arm.

He finally moved, he seemed to be trying to find purchase with his feet. Rub. Bump. Rub. She bit down on her lower lip to suppress a moan. What was wrong with her? Gage finally found footing and pulled away. *Thank god!* Still holding her tightly with that one arm, he hoisted her higher up so that they could both breathe a silent sigh of relief. She tightened her legs around him once more. Anchoring herself above his hips. Holding on for all she was worth. They began to descend again, slowly and carefully. Painstakingly so. Her back knocked or scraped against the odd rock. She wasn't going to get out of this completely unscathed but hey, at least she'd be alive. It took several minutes to negotiate the final ten or twelve feet.

At long last, they made it to the ground. Gage didn't stop to untie her. Instead, he wrapped one arm around her middle, the other secured tightly under her ass. His hand closed on her thigh. He moved quickly, taking big, silent strides. It wasn't long before the towers were in the distance.

"I can walk," she whispered.

Gage nodded, finding a fallen log to sit on so that they could untie themselves from one another. "I'm going to shift. You need to ride me."

"You really do prefer to have the woman on top." *Shit! What the hell!* Why did she have to have such a big trap?

"On top." He chuckled softly. "You would be wrong on that note, sweets."

Edith begged for the ground to open up and swallow her whole but since it didn't happen, she needed to backtrack and fast. "I'm sorry. Again, with another stupid joke." She shook her head. "I guess I'm still a little nervous."

"You did good. Better than good, you did great. It took real guts to get through that. You're allowed to feel unsettled." He looked away for a second before locking his eyes with hers once again. "Sorry about earlier when..."

Oh shit! He wanted to bring that whole embarrassing moment up. "Forget about it," she blurted, waving her hand. Truth was, she'd reacted just as much as he had, only his reaction was a lot harder to hide.

He nodded. "We need to make good time, put some distance between them and us. They might be big, bad and fast, but they can't see at night for shit. Right now, it's our only advantage and I plan on cashing in on it."

"Yeah, you're right. That griffin seemed to be looking our way. It was too dark at that distance, but it looked like it was looking straight at us. It would have sounded the alarm if it knew we were escaping. Do you really think they'll come after us?"

She couldn't make out his features because it was too dark, but she saw him straighten up, his frame becoming rigid. "They took you for a reason. They're not simply going to let you go." He shrugged. "It doesn't matter because we're going to assume the worst. We're not taking any chances."

She nodded.

"Let's get going," Gage said. "We can talk some more later. It's going to be tough going. Let me know if you need a break. We can't stop too often though, we need to get as far away as we can."

"Okay. How far until we get back to your village?"

"I'm not sure." She heard him sniff the air. "I think we're days away from the village. Possibly longer. I'll take care of you, so don't worry."

"I won't."

He turned and took a step away.

"And, Gage..."

He looked back. She could just make out his features. "Thank you."

"You can thank me when we get back safely."

She nodded once, watching as he shifted.

CHAPTER 9

G age could feel that the female was tiring. Her legs didn't hold as readily as before, and she'd even started to slip to the side from time to time in the last while. They had been on the run for a couple of hours and she had yet to signal to him that she was tired. She was though, that much was clear. It was definitely time for a break. All he could say was that he greatly respected her tenacity and determination. She hadn't complained at all through this entire ordeal.

Not even when he'd put his hard as nails dick all over her. *Fuck!* How the hell it had happened in the first place was beyond him. He'd warned her, but he'd never actually believed he'd grow himself a hard-on in a situation like that. Never in a million fucking years. They were so close to being captured, and yet his cock had still been game. Shit, feeling her soft body against him. Hearing her little pants – she was scared fucking shitless, but his body had taken it the wrong way. His body had decided she was turned on and he felt like a colossal asshole pervert for thinking it, for reacting to it. If he could slap himself upside the head, he would.

After everything she had been through at the hands of those creatures, he'd still put her through that. It was wrong. Sure, he could scent that she hadn't been used by them against her will. That she hadn't been forced to have sex with anyone, but still. It didn't mean nothing had happened. That she hadn't been traumatized. He was such an asshole. *Fuck!* Thing was, he hadn't been able to help his reaction. Such a sweet, soft female pressed against him, her legs wide, heat resonating from between her parted thighs. *Stop, Gage! Just stop!* He was still thinking along those lines, still being a perverted fuck. He knew better. It was stopping now. Gage planned on being the perfect gentleman until he got her home. He would see to all her needs and carry her to safety. He vowed it as surely as he had vowed to protect her in the first place.

Guilt ate at him. He'd had to leave Alice and the children behind. He pictured little Ethan and his heart ached for the little boy. What the hell was he going to tell Ash? How was he going to face his brother? He'd drop the human off and head straight out with a team. That's how he would do it.

Feeling marginally better, he looked around them. They were deep in the forest, a thick canopy above them. He was sure they would be safe under the cover of both trees and darkness, at least, for the moment. Gage stopped moving. He felt Edith's body give a jolt and she made a startled sound. She may have been falling asleep and his halt had woken her. He made a growling noise.

"What is it?" Her voice was strained. "What's wrong?"

With a soft rumble, Gage lowered himself, careful not to move too quickly. He didn't want her to fall.

The female got the message and slid off his back. "Thank god," she mumbled to herself.

Gage sucked in a deep breath, concentrating on his human form and shifted. He stretched his arms above his head. "Let's rest for a few minutes." He glanced at her.

By the way she looked in his direction, but not at him, he could tell that she couldn't see very much in the dark. She chewed on her lower lip, doing a careful half turn. "I need to use the bathroom, but I'm scared to take even one step."

"I can see very well in the dark. I'll help you."

Her face looked a tad panicked. "I don't need help, not with going to the bathroom." She sounded a tad panicked too.

"Relax! I'll lead you to a suitable place, I don't plan on sticking around to wipe your ass or anything."

She smiled and rolled her eyes, looking somewhere over his right shoulder instead of at him. "I don't need that kind of bathroom break, thank you very much." Her smile widened.

"That's a good thing because I really hadn't planned on actually wiping your ass for you." *Now, spanking your ass, on the other hand... Stop it!* Gage touched the side of her arm. "I'm going to stand in front of you. Put your hands on my hips and follow me. I don't want you stubbing a toe or tripping over a root and hurting yourself."

After a couple of seconds of waiting she huffed out a breath, sounding frustrated. "I can't see anything. I mean, I can see when you move but not much else. You know that right?" she went on without pausing to take a breath. "I would appreciate a little help with where to place my hands. I can't see where your hips are. I mean, unless you want to accidentally get groped."

Hell yeah! That woke his dick back up; it lifted its perverted head at the prospect of a groping by this female. He really needed to stop this. Gage tamped down on his need to fuck Edith. It was inappropriate and wrong on every level. He wasn't a horny teenager anymore, dammit. A semblance of his control restored, mostly, he reached behind him, taking one of her hands and placing it on his hip and then doing the same with the other. "Ready?"

She murmured an acknowledgment and he set off for the clearing to the side of them. It was slow going. The forest was dense. The brush thick. He lifted a branch or two along the way, so she didn't bash her head. They finally made it to the clearing. It was a good couple of square feet, so she wouldn't end up hurting herself. "This should do it. I'll head back to where we were. You can call me when you're done."

"No looking!"

"Because watching a female pee is on my bucket list." *What an asshole thing to say.*

Her eyes darted to the left before moving back to where he was standing. "I didn't mean…"

He pushed out a heavy breath. "I know. It's been a long-ass night and it's about to get longer," he said, using a much softer tone.

She nodded.

"Call me when you're done," he said, watching as she turned around. Gage walked away, taking care of his own business a good distance away. It wasn't long before Edith called to him and they returned to the path they had been on. It was an animal track and would most likely lead them to water. He hoped it would, at any rate.

"Sit over here," he advised her, turning around and positioning her by holding her upper arms. "There is a big tree behind you for you to lean against. We can't stop for long so make it count."

"Yeah, I know." She leaned back, winced and shot forward, leaning her elbows on her thighs.

Gage frowned. "What is it?" There was something wrong with her back.

"It's nothing." She tried to sound casual.

"No, really, did you hurt yourself?"

"Just some bruising from when my back hit that tower earlier." He could see that she was working hard at sounding nonchalant about the whole thing. Gage wasn't buying it.

He clenched his jaw. "Are you in any pain?" There was an urgency to his voice. "I don't scent blood. Let me see."

"I'm fine, really."

"It's my job, *right now*," he quickly added. "to take care of you. I would really like to take a look."

Edith nodded, leaning forward a bit more. "It's not that bad. The fur helped protect me or I might have been scratched quite badly." She unknotted the animal pelt and let it fall to the ground. Then she pulled her shirt up at the back.

Gage went down on his haunches next to her, he pulled the shirt up a little higher so that he could get a good look. Spread across her skin were red welts and markings, particularly across her shoulder blades and just above the band of her jeans. "I'm so sorry." He shook his head, touching one of the marks.

Edith tried not to react, but he caught her slight flinch. "I'm fine," she quickly said, her voice upbeat.

"No, you're not. Are you sure you can travel? You should have told me about this."

"It's a couple of bruises. Does it hurt a little, especially when touched? Yeah. Am I in any danger? No! Do I need bed rest? Hell no."

Gage pulled her shirt back down. "You're sure?"

"Very."

"You're strong for a human. I'm sorry that happened."

"Not your fault. You're a good climber, for a bear." She smiled.

Gage found himself smiling back. Then he was reminded of where they were and what they were running from. "Tell me what happened with those beasts."

"The griffins?" She raised her brows.

"Yeah, the griffins."

"Good thing you're naked, by the way." Her smile grew.

"How so?" It wasn't like that. Her question certainly wasn't what he was thinking. His cock had it all wrong all over again. Gage took a seat next to her, folding his arms over his lap so she wouldn't somehow develop night vision and catch an eyeful of his growing member. The little-perverted shit. He was beginning to irritate the fuck out of his own self.

"It's a good thing you're in your birthday suit because, well, you did say you would roast your dick over an open fire if these creatures turned out to be griffins."

He choked out a laugh. "I did, didn't I?"

She nodded. "You sure did."

"I would appreciate it if you would let me off the hook. Sounds painful."

"You rescued me, so I guess I could be convinced to do that."

They sat in silence for a few seconds. "What did they want with you?" he finally asked.

"I'm sure you can guess. What is it that men normally want women for?" Her voice was strained. Then she huffed out a breath. "Sorry, that was wrong of me."

"No, it…"

"Yeah, it was." She turned to him. "Not all men are the same. It was unfair of me to make a statement like that."

"After what happened earlier, I don't blame you. I…" He ran a hand through his hair. "I'm so sorry. I don't know how that happened. It shouldn't have happened. It was nothing personal. You need to know that. It didn't mean anything. It just… happened and it's inexcusable. I wish I could take it back." He forced himself to shut the hell up.

"It's okay. Really. Can we drop it?" She looked hurt. Why was that? Then again, it made sense. She was probably reliving the whole thing. The abduction, those dickhead griffins, what happened with him, all of it. His involvement in her discomfort made him want to hit something. He'd save his anger. Save his strength for when he needed it.

"What happened with those griffin fuckers?" His voice was a rough, angry rasp. "I need to know everything. It'll give me a better understanding of them and why they are doing what they are doing. I also need to stay one step ahead of them in the coming days."

She spent the next few minutes taking him through her ordeal and everything that had gone down. "Their females all died?"

"Yes." She nodded. "It sounds like they've been watching you guys... the shifters. They also want humans to take as mates. They want children."

"Aren't they worried about human women also catching whatever it is their own females died from?"

She shrugged. "They don't seem to care. I'm pretty sure Meredith has been tested for... compatibility. That's what they called it."

Gage cursed under his breath. "You're saying one or more of them has... has..."

"Don't say it." Edith swallowed hard. She wrung her hands together. "I can't even begin to think what she's going through. They said she is alive and unhurt, but I find that hard to believe. That one guy – Soren – said she was too small. He was referring to her anatomy when he said it. Apparently, she'd been tested as a potential mate for the king and they found her to be too damned small. It makes me so angry to think about it."

"The fuckers!" he snarled. "That poor female." Guilt rushed through him. Truckloads of the stuff. "This Leukos fucker wanted to mate you? Impregnate you?"

"Yes. They mentioned that I'm..." He watched as her cheeks heated.

"You're what?" he half-growled, then forced himself to calm down. "You can tell me," he added, using a softer tone.

"He said that I was better suited to become one of their mates."

"How so?"

"I'm sturdier. That's the term they used." He could see that she didn't like having been called that. Edith snorted. "I have bigger boobs and hips, so they automatically assumed I'm bigger everywhere, if you know what I mean."

"They were getting ready to test you as well?" There was a hard edge to his voice, he couldn't help it. Goddamn motherfuckers! If he got his hands on one of them... he would probably die but he would take the bastard with him.

"I think so. The king wanted me for himself. That, or I had to choose one of his warriors. They were not going to let me go. I asked several times." She shook her head.

"What I don't understand is what they want with mated females."

She shrugged. "Maybe they're that desperate."

"I don't know." That explanation didn't feel right. "Why children? Why an already pregnant female?"

"Now you have me stumped. It doesn't make sense. I'm just so glad you got me out of there when you did." She shuddered.

"Did they sniff at you?"

"Yes. The king, Leukos, sniffed me. He got down on his knees to do it, getting his nose up close. Too close for comfort." Her eyes were wide. "He then told Soren that I was definitely unmated."

Just as he had thought. "I think their senses are more related to a bird than a lion. They have great eyesight during the day and terrible at night. They have a better sense of smell than a human but not nearly as developed as one of us."

"What does that mean?"

"Like I said, we'll have to travel at night and rest up during the day while they are out searching for us."

Edith nodded.

"I have an idea or two on how to keep them from catching our scent. For one, we need to find the river."

Edith made a soft noise of longing. "I could do with a drink of water."

"I know. How are you holding up otherwise?"

"A soft bed and a deep-dish pizza would be great."

Gage chuckled. "I'll make sure you get both, once we get back. We'll do our best with what we have for now."

"Okay." Again, she didn't bitch or complain.

"One more thing, I have to ask…" He was almost too afraid to do so.

Edith remained silent, her attention on him, although her eyes were trained on his neck instead of his face.

"Did you hear anything about my family? About the pregnant female who was taken?"

Edith nodded. "I asked how everyone was and was told that none of the women or children had been harmed. That they were all in good health."

"I only wish we could believe them."

"I think everyone is still alive, however I think their definition of unharmed might be different to ours."

"Agreed." He sighed. Worry ate at him. Once they

were back, he'd lead a team to rescue the others. He…

Edith touched the side of his arm. "It's not your fault that they're still stuck there. There was nothing we could have done right then to save them."

"I know." Gage clenched his teeth for a moment, allowing her words to sink in. The human was right. "Let's head back out." He needed to push. They were a long damn way from home. Maybe too long.

CHAPTER 10

E dith almost fell off his back but managed to somehow stay on by grabbing his thick fur. She had fallen asleep. Again. Being slumped over his back made it easy to do. In this circumstance though, nodding off was dangerous; next time she might fall off.

Gage lifted his massive head, his top lip curled from his teeth and he made a growling noise. She had no idea what he was trying to tell her. She only hoped it was that they would be stopping soon. It felt like they had been at it for hours and hours. Her muscles burned. The insides of her thighs felt chafed. The muscles on her arms shook. Even her butt hurt. She didn't want to complain because that would be awful of her. How tired must Gage be? He was carrying her. It was his legs that were working.

She thought she heard something. *Yes!* It had to be. She strained her ears. *Definitely!* It was the wonderful sound of running water. Without a doubt. Her tongue felt like it was sticking to the roof of her mouth and her lips felt so dry they might crack. *Water.*

Gage made another growling sound, different this time. It was the growl he always made before he set off. With renewed strength, she held on more tightly as he took off at a lope. Half a minute later the sound of water was much louder. Right next to them. He loped next to the river for a time before crouching down so that she could climb off.

The moon hung low in the sky and she was sure that the start of the sunrise was apparent on the horizon. Right now, it was a thin white line. The stars still twinkled, only not as brightly as before. On either side of the banks of the river was thick forest.

Edith watched as Gage changed into his human shape. His body folding in on itself. She couldn't quite make out details but could see well enough to get by.

"Come," his voice was still thick and deep. It would stay that way for a few minutes while there were still remnants of the bear he had been just moments earlier. "I'm sure you're thirsty."

Instead of answering him, she went down on her haunches at the river's edge and drank deeply. He joined her and they both drank greedily for a few long minutes. Until her belly felt full and her eyes sleepy all over again. Edith yawned and her stomach grumbled, reminding her how long it had been since she had last eaten.

"I'm going to build us a shelter." He looked towards the horizon. The line was lighter than it had been. He breathed out through his nose. "We don't have much time."

"Can I help?"

He seemed taken aback. She could see him look

upwards, like he was trying to think up something for her to do. "Let me get the basic structure up first. We need to head deeper into the forest where the canopy is thick. First though," he gestured to the river, "we must mask our scent. I don't think they'll be able to pick it up that easily, but just to be sure. I don't want to take any chances."

"I agree." She nodded. "How are we going to do it though?" She frowned.

"Like this." He picked up a handful of what had to be mud and began to rub it all over himself. Even in the semi-darkness, she could make out how it smeared across his skin.

"Are you sure this is necessary?"

"I'm sure. Make sure you get it all over your clothes."

She made a face but didn't argue. "Alright." Edith bent down and rubbed some of the mud across the front of her shirt. Although the weather was mild, the mud was cold and gloopy. She could feel the water from the muck soak into her clothing.

"Layer it on thick," Gage said as he rubbed the stuff onto his face, smearing it into his hair.

"If this is what it takes to keep them off our scent and away from us, then I'm game." She scooped up more of the dark, slightly stinky goop and smeared it over her shirt, her jeans, her sneakers and arms.

"Here," Gage gestured for her to turn around. "I'll get your back."

"Thanks ever so much." She tried not to sound sarcastic and failed. Who could blame her? "If someone told me I would find myself in this situation I would've laughed and laughed."

Gage chuckled as he smeared the mud onto her back using firm strokes.

"Heck, I would've told them if it ever happened that I'd roast my balls over an open flame. Not that I have balls but I'm sure you know what I mean."

"Totally." He openly laughed, keeping his voice low. The sound warmed her and despite the mud soaking her to the bone, dripping from her, she laughed too. She laughed a bit harder as she smeared it onto her own face and hair. "It's a new fashion statement."

"You look great." He swept a strand of sticky hair off her face before turning around. "Mind if I ask you to return the favor?"

The sun was definitely coming up, because she could see his broad back. Each well-defined muscle and his strong shoulders. Thankfully, his ass and lower back were already covered in mud. Her mouth suddenly felt dry all over again. Wow! He was gorgeous. Even covered in mud and all stinky. Edith bent down and scooped up big handfuls of the stuff, rubbing it over his back in even strokes. His broad back felt better than it looked. It was a sin to cover up all that bronzed skin. All those layers of muscle. She ran her hands over his shoulders and down his shoulder blades.

It was only when he began to fidget that she realized she'd been taking her time. Enjoying herself a bit too much. "All done," she blurted, giving him a light slap on the back like one chummy friend might give another.

Gage turned, then reached out and gripped her slimy, muddy hand firmly in his. "So you don't trip or get lost."

She looked down at where their hands met. "The sun is coming up, I should be able to see just fine." She didn't attempt to pull away.

Edith was sure she could make out the remnants of a smile behind all of that muck. "That's why we need to move. Don't let go." He squeezed her hand.

"Okay."

They headed out. Within seconds, she could barely see. It was better than before but only marginally. No wonder he had smiled. He'd been laughing at her for sure. "This sucks," she whispered. "It's freaking dark in here."

"It's perfect. They won't see shit through this canopy," Gage said. Every now and then he would squeeze her hand, bringing her closer to his side, or, he'd grip her hips and usher her in front of him, lifting low branches. He even picked her up once or twice to lift her over a boulder or fallen tree. She didn't need to be able to see to know that he didn't break a sweat when he lifted her. His breathing didn't change at all and he certainly didn't groan like some men had done in the past. She was curvy. Very curvy. Had even been called plump once by a guy she was dating. Edith had dropped his ass in an instant. Not because he'd called her that but because he'd told her she might want to think of dieting. She was happy in her own skin. Happy with her own company. The whole making herself come thing was a bit tedious but she…

There was a loud splintering noise. Way to go Edith. She'd been so in her own head that she hadn't realized that he had stopped walking. Not only that, Gage had let her hand go and had walked ahead. He'd just broken a branch right off a tree. Not a thin, twig-like branch. It was a *branch* branch.

Long and thick, kind of like his thighs. Despite the mud, she could see his muscles bulge and thicken as he worked.

Shit! The sun must really be rising if she could make out his ass, his cock. His muddy, muddy cock. She held back a sigh and forced herself to look away from that particular area. Yep, it wasn't the same doing it yourself. Her last casual hook-up hadn't ended well. She'd developed feelings for Jacob while he had moved onto the next girl and then the next one. Thank goodness she was over that whole business.

Nope, she wasn't going there again, and even if she wanted to, it wasn't like Gage was interested. And if he was, it wasn't like this was the best time to get it on. Dirty, hungry, fleeing for their lives. Nope, bad timing. Good thing too, or she might have been tempted to throw caution to the wind. He was just that hot. She was far more attracted to him than she had been to Jacob. She had grown to like Gage too. *Nope! Bad idea!*

Gage's muscles bunched as he lifted the big branch, placing it against a tree. There were more snapping and ripping sounds as Gage went through the same process several times before positioning the branches against a lower hanging bough. It ran vertically to the ground. He placed each leafy limb on either side of the vertical one, forming a natural shelter. It reminded her of a long triangular tent.

Then Gage pulled pieces of brush from some nearby bushes, putting them against the branches to try to seal up the openings.

Edith got down on her hands and knees and entered the shelter. The ground was hard dirt. There were a couple of small rocks inside which she took out one by one. Space was tight in there. Then she picked up leaves, moss, pine needles, any type of soft flooring, and started to place them inside the shelter as a make-shift bed.

Gage finished what he was doing and helped her. In truth, he ended up doing almost all the work. It didn't stop him from giving her a chummy, flat-handed tap on the back. "Good job," he said with a smile. "We'd better hunker down and get some sleep." He gestured for her to go in first. Following behind her.

Things really were tight in the close confines of the shelter. She couldn't move without touching him. Her arm against his. Her knee on his thigh. "Sorry," she murmured.

Gage reached out and pulled her against him, he turned around so that she spooned him from behind. Well not exactly. Her knees touched his thighs but otherwise there was an inch or two of space separating them. "It's going to happen anyway," he said.

"You're probably right." Her voice was a little shriller than she would have liked. "I mean, in a small space like this. We'll be asleep anyway, so it won't count. Not really."

"Exactly. You do whatever you need to get comfortable." He moved, trying to find a more comfortable position himself. "We need to be really quiet though."

"I take it you don't snore then." *Stupid, stupid joke.*

"I hope not. You'll have to let me know. Wake me up if I do." She could hear he was smiling.

"Ditto."

"You snore?" He sounded amused.

"Only if I'm bunged up with the flu, so I think we're good."

"Sleep well." Gage shifted his position again, putting his hand under his head.

"You too." Edith felt wide awake. It was ridiculous. She'd spent the entire night wishing she could lie down and sleep and now that she was... Crickets. The Sandman was nowhere in sight. She was too aware of the big man laying right in front her. His warmth. His presence. It had been a very long time since she slept with a guy. As in, closed her eyes and actually fallen asleep. What if she *did* snore? What if she let off gas? What if...?

Edith started awake, almost hitting her head on the low, branch ceiling. Her back hurt. Her legs hurt. Everything hurt but not in a bad way, in an 'I'm alive and well' kind of a way. Her muscles protested when she reached over, tentatively feeling for Gage. He wasn't there.

She got onto her hands and knees and shuffled to the opening. Her face felt itchy. The mud had dried. She could feel it cracking as she moved. She could just make out the trees and bushes. What time was it?

It couldn't still be morning. Despite her sore, stiff body, she felt refreshed. Like she'd slept for hours on end. Her stomach grumbled, loudly. She put a hand to her belly. Gage would be back soon.

In the meanwhile, she carefully navigated a safe distance from the clearing and took care of business. It was definitely getting darker because she tripped a couple of times and stubbed her toe on the way back. That meant that she'd slept the whole day. How was that possible? Then again, it did make sense, considering she'd been awake for twenty-four hours of hell.

She was tempted to try to make it to the river to clean up and to have a drink but didn't dare for fear of getting lost or hurting herself. Forget the griffins, there had to be wild animals in the forest. Edith hunkered down at the opening of the shelter to wait.

Within fifteen minutes, the woods were pitch black. She could barely make out her hand right in front of her and then only when she moved it. Where was Gage? He should have told her if he was going to leave her like this. She pushed down her frustration. It wouldn't help them. He must surely have a good reason for leaving her.

There was a rustling noise to the right. Her eyes were wide, but she couldn't make out jack shit. Her heart raced. Adrenaline pumped. She had no idea what it was. Could be a small nocturnal animal but it could also be a cougar or a wolf. Not the shifter kind, but the real kind. The kind that would kill and eat a woman without batting an eye. She was a sitting duck. Easy prey.

Forget that.

Edith fumbled around the edge of the shelter, until she felt one of the smaller branches and snapped it off. It didn't come off right away, she had to bend it backwards and forwards, twisting it round and round until it came off. Then she sat at the entrance to the shelter, stick in hand. She would use it as a weapon. Granted, it wasn't a very good weapon, but she'd go down fighting.

Half an hour later and she was shivering. Not because it was cold, rather because it was damn scary out there. Sweat gathered on her brow; the dried dirt was probably turning into mud again. Every now and then she heard a rustling or the snapping of a twig. She tried to sit still, to stay as quiet as possible. As prepared as possible.

Something moved in front of her and she swung, connecting with something, only the something was holding onto the stick. *What?* "Good thing I have such good reflexes. I'm letting go, please don't try to brain me again."

"Gage?" *Oh, thank god!* Her relief turned to irritation. "Don't sneak off like that and don't sneak back like that either. What were you thinking? I thought you were a bear or a cougar or something."

He chuckled. "I *am* a bear."

"You're a shifter who happens to be a bear. Not a real bear, one that would eat me."

Gage didn't say anything. She was beginning to think he'd left again, snuck off, when he cleared his throat. "I won't eat you." he grumbled the words, like he was irritated. "You're perfectly safe. No predator would dare come anywhere near here."

"How do you know that?"

"They would be able to scent me. I pose too great a risk." She could hear him doing something.

"When do we head off?"

"Soon." There were more noises as he carried on with whatever he was busy with. Gage made a grunting noise. "I'm going to start us a fire and then we'll cook dinner. Once we've eaten, we'll hit the road. How does that sound?"

Food. Her mouth salivated just thinking about it. "Sounds fantastic. What's for dinner? I'll eat pretty much anything."

It sounded like Gage faltered. The noises started up

again and a spark flared, followed by another few sparks. Then Gage was blowing on embers which became flames. Next thing, a couple of small sticks and twigs were catching light and he was adding bigger ones.

"Aren't you worried we'll get caught if we light a fire?"

"I don't think so. We need to keep the fire as small as possible. The canopy should contain most of the light." He added a couple more sticks. His skin gleamed golden as the light from the fire flickered against it. Gage was on his knees. He was something alright. Tall, dark and handsome took on a whole new meaning with him around. He turned to her. "You okay?" He frowned. "Your heart-rate went up."

"I'm fine." *Oh shit!* "Just really hungry and looking forward to… Wait a minute. Wait just a minute! You're clean." She pointed at him. "How did you get so clean?"

"I went fishing." He twisted around and picked up two decent-sized fish.

Edith squinted. It looked like they had been gutted. They still had their heads and tails on. They were also still raw, but boy did they look delicious. Her stomach grumbled and she groaned. "Those look so good."

Gage grinned. He put the fish back on the rock behind him.

Edith looked down at herself. Not that she could see anything since she was beyond the reach of the firelight. She knew what she would look like if she could see. She was sure she didn't smell all that good either. She wished she had something clean to change into. "Um, is there time for me to clean up a bit? Maybe you could take me to the bank of the river and then fetch me in ten or fifteen minutes?"

Gage frowned. "I understand that you want to clean up but I'm not leaving you on your own in the open." He threw a few thicker pieces of wood into the fire. "This will take about twenty minutes before it's ready to cook on. I'll take you now." He stood up to his full height. She tried not to ogle him, reminding herself that he could see her perfectly. He'd notice her eyeballs all over him. He'd definitely see the drool.

He walked over to her and helped her up. She probably made a groaning or a grunting noise as she came to her feet because he instantly stilled. "Are you okay? How are you feeling?"

"I'm a little sore and a lot stiff but I'll be fine once I get moving."

"You sure?" His voice was soft, filled with concern. She was certain his features would mirror his tone.

"Yes." She smiled. "I'm very sure."

"It might be quicker if I carry you on my back. Also, I don't want you hurting yourself."

She nodded. "Okay. That's fine."

"I'm on my knees in front of you. Hop on."

She reached out her hands, feeling the top of his head. His hair was soft. She could run her fingers through those strands all day. She forced herself to feel lower, to his neck and then to his strong, broad shoulders, which she gripped.

"Get on my back," he said, his voice a touch gruffer than it had been earlier. Maybe it was her imagination though.

"I must warn you, I'm covered in dirt and I might stink."

"Just get on," he said. "Trust me, you don't stink."

He was just being nice. "And I was told you shifters are supposed to have a good sense of smell."

She thought she heard him mutter something about chocolate and honey – perhaps he was hungry. It couldn't be the way he thought she smelled because that was insane. Mud and sweat… absolutely. Honey and chocolate? She shook her head.

Edith wrapped her arms around his chest and secured her legs around his waist, trying not to get too close and personal. Gage put his arms around her thighs, reminding her of how they used to give each other piggy-back rides as children. Next, he rose to his feet and began walking. It took a good couple of minutes before she heard the sound of running water. They broke from the forest and made their way to the bank.

Gage put her down. Her sneakers squelched in the mud. "Thank you. You really don't have to hang around. I'm going to take a quick dunk." Her hair felt clumped together with mud. "Pity I can't wash my clothes." There was more light out there; she looked down, grimacing at herself before locking eyes with him.

Gage shook his head. "They wouldn't dry. I don't want you getting sick." He paused, seeming to think things over. "I can't leave you. It's too dangerous."

"Okay then," she widened her eyes. "You can turn around. I'll call out if anything goes wrong."

"No, I'm really sorry but I need to stay close."

"How close? Why can't you turn around?" She knew she sounded like a whiner, but in this instance she felt justified.

"I need to come in with you, stand right next to you,

and I can't take my eyes off of you for one second."

"Okay, let me get this straight…" She took a deep breath. "I need to take my clothes off and you have to watch?

"I'm sorry, but yeah, that's right." He looked sincere. Like he felt really bad. He also looked resolute.

CHAPTER 11

Yet again, he felt like a perverted fuck. This was becoming a habit he didn't particularly like.

Gage wished to god he didn't feel so damned excited about watching her undress. Watching her bathe. He was an asshole of note. "I'm sorry!" he said it again, meaning it whole-fucking-heartedly. "Thing is, one of those bastards could come and get you. I don't mind leaving you for a short period under the thick canopy, in the shelter but out here in the open is different. You'd be gone before I could turn around."

"Right now? It's night time." She looked up at the sky. Black and sprinkled with stars. "I thought they couldn't see at night."

"I'm pretty sure they can't but we can't be completely sure." He couldn't take that chance. Wouldn't risk it. "The current is pretty strong as well. What if you were swept away and hurt, or drowned, before I could get to you?"

"Mr. Doomsday."

"I'm serious. I won't risk your life. I'll try to keep my eyes averted as much as possible." As much as his perverted mind would allow.

"Yeah, yeah. It's nothing personal." She made a face. "You guys all walk around naked, so I guess it's normal?" She raised her brows, looking at him expectantly.

Gage didn't say anything. There was nothing remotely normal about how this female would look naked. He couldn't reassure her on that note.

She went on when he didn't say anything. "And it's not like you're attracted to me or anything." She laughed. It sounded like she was a bundle of nerves. He couldn't blame her. Felt like even more of an asshole.

The best course of action was always to be straight with someone. It had never failed him before. "I won't lie, you're a very attractive female. I find you highly desirable, but I won't look more than what is necessary. I won't respond in any way that is inappropriate."

"Really?" Her eyes flared for a second. "You're attracted to me?"

"Why is that so shocking?"

Edith shrugged. "I don't know. I guess… I don't know. Okay. Wow! I…" Her heart was beating overly fast. Like it had been earlier when she'd been checking him out. Her eyes had flitted to his dick a good couple of times and it had taken some serious willpower not to let the little fucker take over. This female was attracted to him too. A recipe for disaster if he ever saw one.

"Like I said, I wouldn't act on it. Would never…" He shook his head a little too vigorously. "It would be a bad idea on every level. Out here." He looked around them. "Being hunted down by those beasts. We can't do anything about it."

"Yep, it would be a terrible idea."

"We'd better get moving," he said, his voice gruff. "We don't want that fire to die out. Also, we need to hit the road soon if we want to make good ground tonight. I'm sure they will know we are following the river. We need to get as far as possible from their territory if we are to stand a chance of escaping them."

Edith moved a few paces away from the water's edge, to where the ground was firm and dry. "Right." She removed her shirt. Then the top underneath. The skin that had been covered by the garments was milky white. The contrast between all the dried up, flaking mud and that clean, soft skin was a turn-on. He was a perverted fuck.

She was gorgeous all bathed in moonlight and white lace was his new favorite thing. No… he gulped… white lace on Edith was his new favorite thing. He bit back a groan.

Eyes up. Eyes up!

Her breasts were a thing of utter beauty. So soft. Gage knew they would bounce. They would feel wonderful in his hands. Her nipples would harden as he sucked on them. *Fuck!* His cock was hardening up. Hopefully she wouldn't be able to see in this light.

He forced himself to look somewhere above her head as Edith toed off her sneakers, stuffing her socks into the shoes. Then she removed the jeans. Good god, those legs. Those thighs. That lace-clad snatch of fur.

Eyes up. Eyes up!

"Mind if I turn around?" Even her smile was as sexy as sin.

"Not at all," his voice was a rough rasp. His dick was close to becoming a full-blown erection. He had zero control.

Eyes up… eyes… her ass was another thing of utter beauty.

"Are you staring at my rear?"

"Maybe. Not anymore. Sorry!" *Shit! What was wrong with him?* "You have a great ass," he blurted. *Why not just tell her you wouldn't mind getting her on all fours?*

She laughed. What a beautiful sound. He really was turning into a pussy. Perverted and pussified. Not the best combination. She folded the jeans and placed them on the ground. "I may have looked at your ass on a couple of occasions, so I guess this makes us even. I'm keeping my G-string on," she said in a sterner tone.

"Good idea," he growled the words. His balls felt heavy. That, and tight. Just about lodged in his damn throat.

She reached behind her back and unclasped her bra. "Can you take this? Please put it on the pile with the rest of my things." She wrapped an arm around her breasts, still facing away from him. *Thank fuck!*

"Sure." If his voice grew any deeper, he might no longer be comprehensible. Couldn't be helped though. Not while standing so close to an almost naked Edith. One sliver of lace. He could slip that out of the way with just one finger. Could be inside her in seconds. She'd be hot and tight. It was a given. His cock throbbed in time with his pulse, which was a tad on the fast side.

Gage took the garment from her, feeling the soft lace

between his fingers. "So, you and Jacob?" *Where the fuck had that come from?* He cringed. Maybe it was his way of heading this off at the pass. Better that way.

Edith pulled her shoulders back as her spine became more rigid. "There is no Jacob and me."

"Didn't look like it from where I was standing." Now he sounded jealous. He wasn't. "What I meant to say was that Jacob still looked pretty interested to me."

"I went to a couple of those Shifter Nights at the Dark Horse." Instead of saying any more, she waded into the water, putting her arms out to help her keep her balance. Side boob was one of the sexiest things ever invented. *Do not look, pervert!*

Eyes up!

It hurt, but he managed to lift his gaze as he waded in after her, staying a few feet away.

"Are you looking?" She sounded amused.

"No. I was, but now I'm not. I swear I'm doing my best here." His best wasn't good enough. Had to try harder.

Edith shrieked as she cupped a handful of water over herself. "It's cold and you were right, the current is strong. I don't want to go in any deeper." The water was up to about mid-thigh. Fuck, even gooseflesh looked sexy on this female.

"Be careful," he warned. "I can hold onto you if need be."

"I think I'll manage." She was definitely smiling.

"I don't mean that in a rude or weird kind of way."

"I know." She made another strangled noise as she dipped down a little into the swirling dark water.

"Funny." He folded his arms, trying not to watch as she began to clean herself in earnest. "I can't picture you in a seedy bar like the Dark Horse."

"Why not?"

"You seem too classy to frequent a pick-up bar like that."

"I'm a red-blooded woman, just like any other."

"I guess so." Shit! He was jealous of Jacob. Of a male who was practically still half-whelp, god help him. "How long ago were the two of you an item?"

She snorted. "We were never an item. It was only one night. Not even a night. Jacob dropped me off in the very early hours of the morning."

He choked out a laugh. "Pup! The male is still wet behind the ears. Couldn't even handle a female for a whole night." Okay, that came out sounding more than a little jealous. He needed to get a handle on this. His dick was seriously getting in the way of his thinking. "All I'm saying is that Jacob seems keen on picking up where the two of you left off."

She bent right over and stuck her head into the water, scrubbing vigorously. Edith came up for a deep breath and went back under.

Fucking pervert that he was, he couldn't seem to take his eyes off her ass. Up in the air. Two white globes of perfection. *No! No!* He looked away. Muttering a curse.

"What was that?" She was slightly out of breath.

"Nothing," he mumbled.

"I must say, I had a bit of a crush on Jacob after our night together." She wrung her hair out. "I tried to meet up with him again, but he wasn't interested. Sure, we'd talk and laugh and then he'd leave with someone else. I eventually stopped going. Look, it happened months ago. It's over and done with."

That's not what Gage had seen. The way Jacob had stared at Edith was telling. His offer to carry the female even more so. "Did you know that Jacob's name has come up on the list? He is eligible to take a mate. Not only that, he's actively looking for one." The young wolf had his sights set on Edith, Gage could feel it. It was none of his business.

"Oh." She didn't seem very interested, but he could be mistaken. "What about you?"

"What about me?" He frowned.

"Is your name on the list?" She didn't mean it like that. She really didn't. Even if she did… nah, she didn't. Thank fuck because… no… just no. It wasn't Edith.

"No!" he said a little too harshly.

"Why not?" She wrung her hair out a second time.

"I haven't gotten around to putting it on there. I had a bad experience with a female – my own fault – and I guess it put me off for the longest time. I have trouble committing."

"But you're ready now?" She glanced back at him from over her shoulder. Her lashes were glistening with water droplets.

Gage swallowed hard. He shrugged. It was a question he'd asked himself a couple of times in the last few weeks. "Maybe. I'm not sure."

Edith turned around. She turned around, dammit. Her hair was wet about her shoulders. Water dripped down her body. The lacy G-string went from sheer to barely there. Both of her arms were wrapped around her breasts which played peek-a-boo from between her forearms. They were just that full. His only salvation was that her nipples were covered. *Jesus!*

"Um, eyes up here, mister."

"Fuck! I'm sorry. I keep doing that."

He watched as her gaze moved to his cock. His very erect, jutting cock. He was damned if the perverted fuck didn't give a twitch. Not only was she sweet, strong-willed and sexy as hell, but she was forward as well. Such great qualities in a female. Gage put a hand over himself. "Um... yeah... well."

"Don't apologize!" She locked eyes back with his and began to walk, he stepped backwards for every step she took until they were on the bank. "It's this whole situation. We're dependent on one another. Like you said before, it's not personal." She turned, facing away from him. Using the spaghetti-strapped top, she began to wipe herself off. Then she put the bra back on. Followed by the T-shirt.

His balls actually clenched when she took off the lacey G-string. Her shirt came to just below her ass, so he couldn't actually see anything. Not that he was looking. Even though he wanted to. He'd love to catch a glimpse of her naked pussy. His cock throbbed, his balls clenched so tight that with just a couple of firm tugs, he'd be tickets. Who was he to call Jacob wet behind the ears?

There was so much at stake.

They in the middle of no-fucking-where being hunted by griffins. Big-ass mothers who could take him out and do whatever they wanted to the human. There was no doubt in his mind what they had in mind for her and it wasn't pretty. Then there was Jacob and the fact that there was something going on between the two of them.

He'd been in the middle of a love triangle before and it wasn't fun. It had almost cost him his relationship with his brother. Had almost destroyed him.

Then, on top of all that, there were innocent females and children whose lives were solidly in his hands and here he was getting all amorous. Thinking with his dick instead of his head. His mind so far off the game it was scary.

"We need to move." It was like someone had doused him in freezing water. "I have to apologize for my behavior. I don't normally have to apologize for the same thing over and over. It won't happen again and this time I mean it."

"It's fine." Edith was looking down as she hurriedly tied her laces, using jerky movements. He got the feeling he'd said the wrong thing again. That she was mad at him.

"That smells so good." She watched as Gage turned the fish like a pro. "Where did you learn how to cook?" She ran her hands through her hair, thankful she'd cut it not so long ago. She dreaded what was going to happen when it dried completely.

He shrugged. "I go on regular scouting trips, either with other males or solo. We take turns cooking."

"I thought you would just hunt something down and go crazy on the kill."

Gage smiled. "On occasion, but our human side is more dominant. We spend more time in our skins then our furs, so it stands to reason we prefer being civilized."

Oops! "Sorry. I didn't mean that as an insult, I'm simply curious."

"No worries! Ask anything. I don't mind." He looked up from what he was doing and did a double-take. His gaze zoned in on her… *No, please no!*

"Don't say anything! Don't you dare." She pointed at him.

Gage's eyes had this glint. He was smiling… no, make that smirking. "I'm not saying anything. Not a word."

His smirk grew. "Dinner is almost ready. You hungry, Curls?"

Her mouth dropped open. "You didn't just call me that!"

Gage chuckled. "I'm calling it like I see it. Besides, I think you look adorable."

"Adorable? Really?" She folded her arms. "I'm not adorable. Little girls are adorable. I'm a grown woman, last time I checked." She mumbled the last.

His whole expression changed. "I didn't mean to upset you. It was a joke. I happen to think adorable and sexy can go hand-in-hand. Just so you know, there's nothing wrong with having really curly hair. It's a unique trait. It's all you. I like the look." Sincerity shone in his eyes. He held her gaze for a few moments before placing one of the fish on a large, thick leaf and handing it to her.

Oh shoot! Now she felt like a terrible person. "Thank you for this." She held up her fish. It looked delicious. It smelled even better. It didn't need herbs or butter or anything.

"It's a pleasure."

He was so sweet. "Thank you for the food and the nice things you said."

"No need to thank me for that. I shouldn't have teased

you in the first place."

She kind of liked that he had teased her. After hearing the explanation, she kind of liked the nickname too. "You can tease me. You can even call me Curls if you want. I don't mind." She pulled a piece of the fish off the bone and blew on it. "I guess I'm a little touchy about my hair. It's the reason I blow dry it straight. I've even had it chemically straightened a good couple of times."

He frowned but didn't say anything.

"Kids used to tease me at school. They called me Frizzy Lizzy all through junior high."

"Kids can be cruel," Gage said simply. She noticed he wasn't touching his food.

"It got worse, I became Kinky Edith in college. That's when I started straightening my hair. I don't mind a light curl, but this," she ran a hand through her tight curls, "this I hate."

Gage shrugged. "You look like you, whether you have curly hair or straight hair. You're an attractive female, I already told you that. I meant the nickname as a compliment… not in a weird kind of a way though. As friends. I meant it in the best possible way."

"I know." She pushed out a breath. "You don't have to explain. I overreacted. I wanted you to know why I'm a little sensitive. Thank you for saying all that and for making me feel better about something that's bugged me for so long."

"I said it because I meant it."

"I know you did." She licked her lips. "You can call me Curls if you want to."

Gage grinned. "I was going to call you Curls whether you liked it or not."

Somehow, she doubted that.

He winked at her, finally taking a bite of his fish. So, Gage thought she was adorable and sexy, and he was attracted to her. She shouldn't feel happy about this, but she did. She felt all warm inside, and it wasn't just the food that was finally going into her belly. The problem was that Edith would end up being just another hook-up to Gage. Once they got back to reality, it would be over. She knew it as plainly as she knew her own name. Gage had said he wasn't ready for a relationship. That he had commitment problems. His name wasn't even on that stupid shifter list. Edith wanted more. So much more. More than he had to give.

She took another bite, forcing herself to smile. "This is delicious."

CHAPTER 12

THE NEXT DAY...

T he embers of the fire crackled as a piece of skin or fat fell onto them. She could smell the fish roasting. "Are you sure it isn't done yet?"

Gage smiled. "Very sure, unless you want half-cooked food?" He lifted a brow.

"I'll wait." She sighed. "This 'two meals a day' thing is not for me." Then she laughed. "I'm more of a 'six meals a day' girl. Three square ones with a couple of snacks thrown in-between."

Gage bit back a grin. "I'm sorry I'm not providing enough for you," he teased. "If it weren't for the griffins on our tail…"

Her gaze instantly darkened. "You know I don't mean it like that. I know —"

"No need to get so testy, I'm joking." He turned the fish, and it sizzled. "Two more minutes and you'll get your food, Curls."

"Sorry. You probably noticed already, but I'm prone to getting hangry."

"Don't you mean hungry?" He frowned.

She shook her head. "No, I mean hangry, it's a mix between hungry and angry."

"Oh, I see." He laughed. "Yep, that's a perfect description of you when you're hungry."

She pretended to scowl. "Under the circumstances, I think I've been okay. You haven't seen me really hangry yet. I work with a guy named Jeff, and he knows only too well. If I'm in a mood, he orders food, or pops into the coffee shop around the corner for fresh cinnamon rolls." She groaned, making his dick harden. "What I wouldn't give for a cinnamon roll."

"Can't help you there. I'm afraid it's fish on the menu again. Sorry to disappoint."

She made the cutest little snort. "What I wouldn't give for a pastry." She looked wistful for a moment. "Good news is that fish might be my new favorite food." She eyed their meal greedily.

"What do you do for work? And who's Jeff?" There was an edge to his voice he didn't like.

"Jeff is an asshole," she muttered. Why did he enjoy hearing her call him that?

Then she sighed. "That's not entirely true. He's been trying to steal some of my business lately. Sure, he's driven and wants to make money. I should be proud since I trained him." Then she looked him head-on. "I'm a real estate agent." She obviously caught the blank look in his eyes because she went on. "I sell houses for a living."

"Oh, that sounds interesting."

"I enjoy it. Sweetwater is very up and coming. It's becoming a desirable place to live. The real estate business is booming. I just managed to pick up one of the prime lake-front properties and man oh man is it a beauty. The first show day is on Sunday." Her eyes widened. "We will be back before then, won't we?"

Gage nodded, he removed her fish from the heat, placing it on a leaf. "Yes, we will be back before then." He handed her the food.

"Thank you. This looks so good." Edith blew on the fish. Then she glanced up. "I'll tell you a secret…" She looked serious for a moment. "I don't particularly want to sell this property."

"Why not? It's your job isn't it?"

She peeled a small piece of fish off and popped it into her mouth. Edith closed her eyes and groaned. He was fucked if he didn't feel it in his groin, which tightened uncomfortably. He looked down, trying to concentrate on his own meal and not on the look of rapture on her face as she chewed. Gage was glad he'd brought her that pleasure, only he could think of better ways to do it.

"The Jones property is something special."

Human females tended to like material things. He waited for her to tell him how big it was and about the gleaming marble floors.

"I love the feel of the place. The view of the lake is second to none. Then there's the porch. I could picture sitting out on that porch, the sun setting over the lake. Kids playing on the lawn."

"I'm sure it's big and airy."

She giggled. "Who's the estate agent. Me or you?

Actually, it's an older property. Not very big. I would knock down a few walls and put in a couple of bigger windows. It has promise and old charm. I'm so afraid someone with big money will come along and level the place. It's got an old fireplace complete with mantle. The Oregon pine doors are just beautiful." She shrugged. "I'd change a few things for sure, but I'd keep most of it the way it is."

That was a surprise. Then again, Curls was a surprising female. He found that aside from wanting to do dirty things to her, he liked her. Liked her very much. "Why don't you buy the place?"

Edith burst out laughing, slapping a hand over her mouth so that she didn't spray her food. When she was able, she swallowed. "Yeah right. It's prime real estate. I don't have that kind of money. I hope someone who appreciates it will buy it and improve on what's there instead of taking the whole place to the ground."

"I'm sure you'll find the right buyer."

"It's my job to get the right price for the sellers. It's my duty. The Joneses are an old couple. Mister Jones recently retired. They need the money."

Sexy as hell and sweet too. This female was the whole package. She was going to make someone very happy. "You're a good person, Curls."

She smiled at him, the light from the fire brightening her eyes.

THREE DAYS LATER...

There was a crack of a twig. "It's me, Curls," Gage warned. "Don't hit me, please." He chuckled.

Edith smiled and rolled her eyes, putting the stick down. "I told you not to sneak up on me. It's not my fault you didn't listen yesterday."

"I'm still bruised."

"You talk shit," she snickered.

Gage chuckled. It had become a ritual. He would wake her when he left to go foraging, and she would sit outside whatever makeshift shelter they'd built for the night with a stick firmly in her hands until he came back. Gage had told her over and over that no predators would come anywhere near them, but her whole philosophy was rather safe than sorry. She was sticking to it, thank you very much. Hence the noisy approach this evening. She'd cracked him on the shin yesterday. Served him right for sneaking up on her and for his slow reflexes.

"I've got a treat for you," Gage said as he approached.

"Oh! Something I can eat I hope."

He paused and then cleared his throat. "Yep! Something you can eat." His voice was all deep and rough. "Hold out your hand."

She did as he said, and he dropped a handful of something into them. Small, soft and knobby. She sniffed at them, but they didn't give off much of a scent.

"Try one," he insisted.

"What are they?"

"Trust me already and try one." He sounded excited.

She did as he said and moaned as the flavors burst in her mouth. They were juicy and delicious – both tart and sweet at the same time. "That's so good," she smiled, talking around her food. She swallowed and threw a couple more into her mouth.

"What did I tell you? They're wild raspberries."

"I could eat a truckload of these," she gushed.

"That would be a terrible idea."

"Why?" she groaned. "I'm sure they're good for you."

"Take it from someone who knows." She could hear he was smiling. "I ate a ton of those things as a young boy and really regretted it. They gave me severe stomach cramps followed by… you don't want to know… it was ugly."

She couldn't help but laugh. "I'm sorry. I shouldn't laugh at your expense, but I can't help it."

He chuckled. "I wouldn't want you to suffer the same fate. I'm sure we'll find another bush or two en route, just don't eat too many in one sitting. Besides," he breathed out through his nose, "I caught us a nice, fat rabbit."

She clapped her hands. "Sounds delicious." They'd been living on fish for the last few days. Not that she was complaining.

"Rabbit is one of my favorites," Gage said.

"I'm sure I'll be right on board in an hour or two." It was weird how life changed things. Edith had always been a major animal lover. She donated money to several charities and walked dogs at the local shelter on Monday mornings. If her job wasn't so demanding, she'd adopt one or two of her own. If you had told her a week ago that she'd be salivating over a sweet, little bunny she'd have laughed and laughed. Possibly even given you a really dirty look. Right now though, it was the complete opposite. "Do you need some help cleaning it or making the fire?"

"Nah, I'll manage fine. I take it you want to wash up?" he asked, from somewhere to the right of her. She couldn't see much. Just the odd flit of movement in the darkness.

"Yeah, that would be good. I hate the way the mud feels once it's dried and flaking off."

"Itchy?"

"Very," she huffed.

"Let me get the fire going and I'll take you to the river."

"Sounds good."

Gage did as he said. Then he carried her to the water. Like she said earlier, they had a routine going. She waded in and did what she needed to do. Only, unlike that first time, he didn't watch. Didn't eyeball her ass. Or become aroused in any way. He just stayed close, keeping her in his peripheral vision in case anything happened. They'd fallen into something of a friendship. Yet, the sexual tension was still there. Not so much on the surface but simmering just beneath. At least, it was for her. She was doing her best to ignore it, but it wasn't easy. Especially since he was naked all the time. You would think she would become used to his state of undress, but she hadn't. He was that gorgeous. That ripped. That sexy.

"These clothes are disgusting," she said as she dressed.

"What if you washed them and wore the fur?"

"I'm starting to stink, aren't I?" They had no toiletries. They used ash to brush their teeth. *Ash. Argh!* No wonder Gage wasn't looking at her in that way anymore.

"I'm not sure that would work. My thighs might chafe if I rode you in just a fur and my undies." Rode him. *Rode.* Now there was a thought.

"We'll wash your things tomorrow morning when we stop to rest up for the day. Your clothing will, hopefully, dry while we sleep."

That would mean that both of them would be in close confines, naked, or close to naked in her case. Oh! She liked the sound of that. She shouldn't. She really shouldn't, but she did. All cozy, pressed up against one another. Maybe Gage would kiss her. Maybe they would do more than just kiss. She pressed her thighs together. Another casual fling was not what she was looking for.

His nostrils flared and he got this strange look in his eyes. His jaw clenched. Gage looked angry for a second. Not that she could see all that well. She was probably misreading whatever vibe was coming off of him. "Or not," Gage practically growled. He sounded angry. "Maybe it's not such a good—"

"Yes! Please can we do that? Wash my stuff?" She brushed a hand over the disgusting material of her shirt. "Otherwise, mud or no mud, those griffins might be able to smell me. My clothes are that ripe." She giggled.

"I think you're fine but if it will make you feel more comfortable, we'll wash them later."

"Yes, please."

"Come on, Curls. Let's get you back and fed. We need to hit the road. We have another long night ahead."

Edith nodded, warming at his nickname for her. Gage bent down over his knees and she hopped aboard. She was getting good at this too. Riding him. She shook her head at her own stupid joke. Riding him, yeah right, like that was ever going to happen.

CHAPTER 13

LATER THAT DAY...

Someone clamped a hand over her mouth and a strong arm banded firmly around her. Edith was unable to move. She had to let Gage know she was in trouble. Had to do it now! Her eyes were wide. She tried to suck in air through her nose to attempt a scream when she realized it was Gage who held her so tightly. It was Gage with his hand over her mouth. It was his big brown eyes that held hers.

"Shhhh," he mouthed as he slowly released her.

She nodded once, trying to catch her breath. Her heart raced. His eyes lifted to the branches above their heads. He was clearly listening to something she couldn't hear, even though she strained her ears. It wasn't right though. Something was off. She couldn't quite put her finger on what it was exactly.

His jaw tensed and his whole body hardened. His eyes

narrowed.

"Come." Again, he mouthed the word instead of actually saying it out loud. They carefully crawled from the shelter. Gage pulled her to her feet. Her still damp clothing was suspended on one of the lower hanging boughs in the clearing, just to the right of the shelter. She wore her underwear. The fur was still on the floor in the shelter. She contemplated fetching it. Edith was practically naked. Wearing just sheer lace underwear, she may as well be.

Gage gave a sharp shake of the head when she tried to pick up her shirt. He gestured to his back, going down on his haunches. It was still daylight. Dapples of sun shone through the trees. Why had Gage woken them up? What was going on?

He had always insisted that predators would stay away. Gage wouldn't act this way for a predator though. It was them. It had to be. Then she realized what was wrong, the blood drained from her body. It was quiet. Completely silent. No birds singing, no crickets chirping, no squirrels scratching. It was like all the creatures of the forest had gone into hiding. Her hairs stood on edge.

A shadow darted over them. Quick. There one second, gone the next. If she hadn't been looking up, she would have missed it. The canopy was so thick and whoever had made that shadow, moved that quickly. Her heart caught in her throat and her skin felt instantly clammy. Edith gripped his shoulders and jumped onto his back. Gage was running before he secured his arms around her thighs. She gripped tighter to ensure she didn't fall off. The crazy thing was, she was becoming good at this. Surely he should shift? Edith didn't dare ask. He must know what he was doing.

They moved fast and she held on for dear life. Gage seemed to know exactly where he was going, which was weird considering they'd never been there before. At least, she didn't think he'd been to this part of the woods. He hadn't mentioned that they were nearing his village but maybe she had this all wrong.

She glanced up every now and then. Mostly though, she focused on hanging onto Gage. A more apt description was trying not to fall off. Every so often, he would stop, his gaze fixed up ahead. His senses alert. Nostrils flaring. If his ears could twitch they would. Then he would take off running, his focus unwavering. His arms holding her tight. He darted between the trees and the brush, leaping over a boulder or log from time to time.

At one point, he stopped dead, pushing them up against the bark of a large tree. Although his chest heaved, he didn't make a sound. There it was again, that shadow. Slower this time. It was searching for them. Had picked up on something. Their scent maybe? Footprints perhaps?

Shit!

What would happen to Gage if they were captured? They needed her, but they didn't have any use for him. He'd be killed, she knew it as surely as she knew her own name. Probably would've murdered him if they hadn't escaped when they did. She shuddered at the thought. Gage rubbed a hand up and down her thigh a couple of times to reassure her.

Half a minute later and Gage was running again. Faster than before. The threat of danger even closer. It felt like the griffins were closing in. At this rate, they were not going to make it. She tried not to think negative thoughts, but it was becoming more and more difficult.

They arrived at the edge of a large clearing. There was an open section that led to a tall cliff. They would be trapped on one side, or would be soon if Gage didn't move. Instead, they stood in the shadows at the forest edge. Gage scanned the sky. There were a half a dozen questions on the tip of her tongue, but she held them all back.

He tensed, quietly moving back so that they were sheltered behind a large tree. There it was again, that blasted shadow. A griffin. Close. Too damned close for any kind of comfort. She swallowed thickly, trying to control her heart-rate, her breathing. Trying not to make so much as a sound.

It felt like an age before Gage sucked in a deep breath. He made a run for the cliff. Straight for the sheer wall. What was he doing? There would be no place to go. Just scraggy rocks and a sheer cliff surface. There wasn't so much as a bush to hide behind. His footfalls were relatively quiet on the rocky ground. Not as quiet as before. Her heart hammered. Any moment now and they might be spotted. They were sitting ducks out in the open like this.

Thank god!

Edith felt like sobbing with relief when she saw that, between what looked like an overhang, was a large crack in the cliff. It was tall, all the way up to the top, but it was also narrow. It couldn't be more than three or four feet across. Gage bent down, so that she could slide from his back. He turned and gripped her upper arms, pulling her against him. Then he angled them so that they were aligned with the opening. It looked deep.

Breathing heavily, Gage eased them into the narrow space. The two of them could fit, but only just. He shuffled deeper and deeper into the crevice.

Thankfully, she wasn't claustrophobic because she would never have survived this. Not in a million billion years. As it stood, her eyes felt wide. Her blood rushed in her ears. It was incredibly tight and dark. There was a tiny sliver of light above them. The main opening was obscured by rocks. Her chest was pressed against his. Scratch that, every part of him was pressed against every part of her. Gage's skin felt hot. His hands were still clasping the sides of her arms. His chest rose and fell in quick succession, pressing more firmly against her boobs. Her face was chest level to him. She could smell him. Masculine. It was the only word to describe it, to describe him.

There it was again. That blasted shadow. Darkness befell them for a second or two. Not long after, another one flew over. Or was it the same one flying in circles? Had it seen them? Was it closing in?

There was a loud shriek seconds later, followed by an answering shriek from some ways away. More than one then. She shivered and pressed her cheek against his chest, squeezing her eyes closed.

Please don't let them find us! Please!

Gage squeezed her upper arms. Then he cupped a hand behind her head, holding her against him. His fingers threading into her hair. His breath warm against the top of her head. They were in this together and that was something. The thought helped calm her, as the screeching noises grew more and more distant. She wasn't sure whether minutes passed or much longer.

"You okay, Curls?" Gage finally whispered. She felt something press against her head and was shocked to realize that he had kissed her. At least, she was almost one hundred percent sure he'd kissed her on the top of her head.

She nodded, her cheek still resting against his chest. His very beautiful chest.

"I think we should sit tight for a few more minutes," he whispered. "Just to be sure."

"Okay."

"You did good." He was so darned sweet. How could a guy be this good-looking and this kind? He always put her needs first. Could've saved himself and left her a long time ago. To think there was a woman in his past who had hurt him. Unbelievable. He blamed himself, but she was sure that there was more to it. If he was hers... No, that wasn't a possibility, so best she drop that line of thought right now.

"You did good too." She squeezed his bicep. His thick, hard bicep, realizing for the first time that she was holding onto him tightly. One hand curled around his neck and the other held his arm.

He pushed out a heavy breath and when she looked up, he had his head tilted up and his eyes closed. He looked like he was in pain. Had he hurt himself?

Then she felt it. His cock. It was thickening and lengthening. He squeezed his eyes even tighter, gritting his teeth. "I'm so damned sorry," he whispered. His voice deep and beautiful like the rest of him. Beautiful with a double side of sexy.

It was clear that Gage still wanted her as much as that

first day. Edith wanted him too. Maybe more. She wanted him to make her feel alive. To feel free because she was all of those things. They both were. They had survived. More than anything she wanted to just be with him, even if it was only for a few more days at the very most. She didn't want them to keep pushing each other away. Feeling braver than she ever thought she could be, Edith stood up on her tippy toes and kissed Gage on the neck. Right on that spot just below his ear.

He sucked in a deep breath and opened his eyes, looking down at her. His large brown orbs were filled with shock and desire.

CHAPTER 14

One second Gage had been berating himself for being a despicable person. For subjecting Edith to… to… his unwanted advances. Not that he was actually making moves on her. His erection was happening against his will, dammit. He didn't seem to have much control around her. Especially when he was this close to this particular female. Her lace-clad breasts pushed tightly against him. He could scent her, could feel her. He wanted her more than he'd wanted anyone before.

"I'm so damned sorry!" He was such a prick, such a —

Edith kissed him. Kissed. Him. Pressed those soft, pillowy lips against the sensitive skin on his neck. It was the very last thing he expected. His dick hardened all the way up. Stiff against her belly. Gage had to use every last resolve not to tear off her panties and sink himself into her. Although he doubted that it would be possible in this narrow crevice. Too narrow to fuck her properly, at any rate, which was a good thing. It forced them to take the time to think this through first.

When he did nothing, she kissed him again, smiling this time as she came up. It was such a sweet, shy smile.

"Do you want sex?" he blurted, sounding like a damned cub.

Edith swallowed. "Yes. I definitely want sex. Don't you?" Her cheeks had turned a lighter shade of pink.

Gage chuckled softly. "I think you can tell how much I would love to be inside you."

"I'm sensing that there's a *but* in there somewhere."

"I'm not on that list." He shook his head. "I'm not eligible to have a relationship and I'm not sure I'm ready…"

She reached up and put a finger over his lips. "I know and I'm okay with it." Something flared in her eyes that told him she wasn't as okay with it as she thought. They shouldn't do this.

"The whole reason I can't picture you in a seedy pick-up bar is because I see you as someone who wants more. You belong in a relationship with a male who cares for you, who cherishes you."

"Like I said, I'm a red-blooded woman, I have needs. Right now, I need this. We're both consenting adults and we want one another. It doesn't have to become complicated." They were still whispering.

"You're sure?" He frowned.

Edith nodded. "Very sure." She sounded sure. In this moment, she even looked sure. Maybe he was making too big a deal over sex. They were attracted to one another. Big fucking time. Maybe it would be better if they just fucked and got it over with.

Gage leaned in and pressed his lips to hers. Just as soft as they looked. Just as tasty too. He slanted his mouth over hers and deepened the kiss. *Fucking hell!* He could get lost in her. Drown in her. He cupped her chin, demanding that she give him more and Edith rose to the occasion. She mewled into his mouth. Her nipples pebbled against him. He could scent her need.

They couldn't leave this tiny space yet but that didn't mean he couldn't make her come. Gage shuffled past her, leaving one of his thighs between her legs. "Shhhh," he whispered against her lips.

He slid a hand between them, cupping her pussy. *Fucking hell!* Her lace slip was soaking wet. He couldn't help himself when his chest vibrated and a low rumble escaped. His dick gave a lurch, desperate to be inside her. Using two fingers, Gage shoved the fabric aside and slipped his fingers between her folds, zoning in on her clit.

Edith cried out, but he swallowed the sound as his fingers softly circled her bundle of nerves. She arched her back as much as the tight confines would allow, breathing heavily through her nose.

Using the same two fingers, he pushed into her. "So damned wet," he mumbled against her lips. He crooked his fingers a little, zoning in on her g-spot.

By the way her eyes widened and the sound of her sharp intake of breath, he reckoned he'd found it. Using firm, easy strokes, he finger-fucked her, listening as her heart-rate sped up. How her breathing became ragged. So damned sexy.

Just as her pussy began to tighten, he slowed right down, easing off her sweet spot. He moved back to her clit and using one finger, he made lazy circles around the swollen nub. Round and round and round. Her back arched, her eyes closed, her head had rolled back against the stone wall. Edith bit down on her lower lip, holding it between her teeth. She moaned loudly as he slipped back across her clit.

Gage took back her mouth. They needed to be quiet for a little longer, just to be sure. He was still listening for any activity outside. He figured his hearing was better than the griffins', that they were long gone, but he couldn't be too careful. Couldn't lose focus yet.

She kissed him this time, sucking on his tongue and nipping at his lips. His balls pulled tight as he pushed three fingers into her tight as fuck pussy.

"Oh god," she moaned.

Gage stopped moving inside her and pulled away. Her eyes were wide and glassy. Her mouth was glistening and swollen from his kisses. Her cheeks were flushed. Her hair a wild tangle of curls. God, how he wanted her. Even more, he wanted to hear her come loudly. It would have to wait for some other time though. "You need to be quiet, Curls, or I'll have to stop."

"No, please no." She gripped his forearm. "I'll be quiet. I swear."

"You're about to come really hard," he warned.

"Promise." She groaned softly as he began to slowly pump in and out of her again. "Just… so… good," she murmured as he picked up the pace.

Using the pad of his thumb, he rubbed her tight nub. One, two, three times and her face became taut. Her eyes rolled back. Her pussy tightened around his fingers. She clamped her mouth tightly shut. Her hips rocked in tight circular motions as much as the cramped confines would allow. He kept her there for a time before slowing and softening his movements. Edith slumped against him. She was breathing hard. Strands of her hair clung to her forehead.

Gage gave her a few moments to catch her breath. It gave him an opportunity to make sure that they really were alone. That those motherfucker griffins had moved off. The sounds of the forest were back. Otherwise, all was quiet.

Her breathing slowed and she finally lifted her head. Her eyes were still a little hazy. She was smiling. It was about a mile wide and had 'satisfied' written all over it. "I'm good, how about you?" she whispered.

"I'm glad." He brushed a couple of wayward curls from her face. "I'm far from good though. I really need to fuck you now, Edith."

He watched as her pupils narrowed. Lust would do that to a female. *Good!*

"I want inside your tight pussy. I'm going to bury myself so deep inside you that you'll come hard and fast."

She licked her lips. "I'd forgotten how dirty shifters talk."

He felt his jaw tighten. Fuck, everything tightened. He'd forgotten about Jacob and Edith. It didn't matter though. This was just a little fun. He was going to make it his mission to make her body forget Jacob. To make her forget the encounter had ever happened. To make her come harder, faster and more often.

Gage pulled her against him and began to shuffle back out. Then he picked her up and raced for the forest. Once they were a good distance under the thick of the canopy, he put her down on her feet, taking a step away from her so that he could look at her. Actually look at her. Not sneak a sideways glance but really fucking look. Take her all in.

She was curvy in all the right places. Plenty curvy. Tits, ass, hips, belly. She had it all. The white lace was no longer all that white, it was dirtied up. Even that was fucking sexy.

"What?" She suddenly looked self-conscious and even wrapped an arm across her belly and another one across her breasts.

Gage shook his head. "Don't cover yourself. I'm admiring you. I'm looking at everything I'm about to have." He lifted his eyes up to meet hers. "I'm thanking my lucky stars because you are exquisite."

"Oh please." She made a snorting sound. "I'm hardly exquisite. I have good qualities, sure, plenty of those, but I could lose a few pounds and I have some cellulite on my thighs and…"

"Stop. You are all female and you are perfect. I'm not sure what to do with you." He let his gaze track her lush curves.

"I could give you a lesson on the birds and the bees and how things work, but…"

He choked out a laugh, sure to keep his voice down. Just to be sure. "I know how to fuck just fine."

"I'm sure you do." He could scent her arousal. So decadent.

"I want you so badly and in so many ways. On your knees, up against that tree, bent over that boulder. I want you riding me, but I also want you on your back with your legs draped over my shoulders. More than we have time for right now." Just putting it out there because it was good to establish these things up front.

Her irises were like pinpricks. Her breathing labored. "We might have to fuck a few times then over the next couple of days."

Gage nodded. "Good plan. I like the way you think." Although this was a short-term deal, it was more than just a one-time deal. He was infinitely glad. "The bear in me needs you naked and on your knees. Once I've satisfied some base needs, we can play."

"Sounds good to me." She reached behind her back and unsnapped her bra. He felt his eyes bug right out of his head. His jaw dropped open. Her breasts were heavy and yet firm. So damned soft looking. Her aureoles were wide and her nipples tight.

He watched in utter rapture as she removed her panties, stepping out of them, one leg at a time. She had a narrow strip of fur covering her slit. Gage muttered a curse and closed the distance between them. He picked her up against him and kissed her. First on her lips, then her throat. At long fucking last, he took one of those plump nipples into his mouth and sucked softly. Her nipple hardened up even more in his mouth.

Edith moaned. He put her down, but only so that he could palm her other breast. So soft, so full, so lush. "What about protection?" Edith muttered.

It took long seconds for him to register what she had said. He stopped suckling on her chest. "Shit! I knew I was forgetting something." He shook his head. "There have been a couple of accidental pregnancies over the last year or two." He was appalled at the thought of not being able to have her. Of not being able to make her come on the end of his dick. "Considering how much unprotected sex the shifters have had previously, it hasn't happened very often. We are good at predicting if a female is fertile or not. The pregnancies put a stop to unprotected sex. We can't give one another an STD, so that's not a problem."

"I'm on the pill but, yeah…" She raised her eyebrows. "I haven't been able to take that over the last couple of days."

"I don't have any condoms."

"Nope, I don't suppose you do." She gave him one of her beautiful smiles. "That's okay, we can make the most of it." She went down onto her knees in front of him, her gaze on his cock. She cupped his balls with one hand making him groan. He could feel her breath on his tip.

Although the thought of her lips wrapped around his length appealed to him in so many ways, this wasn't how he wanted this to go down. "Wait." He gripped her cheek. "You have no idea how much I would love to watch you suck me off, but I really want to fuck you. What if I pulled out before… before I come?"

"It's not a sure-fire method." She rose to her feet.

"I don't scent your heat… that you are ovulating." He'd heard the human females talking on many occasions. He remembered the terminology. "I will pull out as a precautionary measure. If I scent your heat. Even if I suspect that you are headed that way, I promise I will tell you. We will then have to refrain from having sex. I will get you off with my mouth, although I suspect I might have to taste you regardless. You keep talking about bears eating you. My mind went to the gutter every damn time. This bear would love to eat you." He grit his teeth for a moment. "I would love to make you come while buried inside you, would you be okay with me pulling out?"

Her eyes brightened with excitement. "Okay." She nodded. "As long as you're sure you can pull out."

"I will, I swear. I'm not ready to become a father and I'm sure you feel the same?"

"What, to become a father?" She laughed. "Nope, I'm not ready to become a dad. A mom on the other hand…" She turned serious. "When the right guy comes along. One who's serious about me. Then," she shrugged, "I would be ready. I definitely want children. One day that is," she quickly added the last.

Gage felt both afraid and jealous. Afraid that things might become complicated between them. He was definitely not ready for a relationship. What if he fucked things up again? No, he was sure he would fuck things up. He wasn't ready for anything serious. Yet he was jealous of a male he had never met. The male who would win Edith's heart. He envied him. Wished to god he could be him. He wasn't going to hurt her though. No fucking way.

"What is it?" Edith frowned. "You're all serious all of a sudden."

"Fucking you is serious business. It's a job I don't take lightly." He picked her up and walked over to where soft velvety moss grew under a particularly large tree. He put her down. "Would you mind if I took you from behind?"

"Bear-style?" she teased.

"Something like that, yes." He smiled at her, feeling everything in him tighten with need.

"Sign me up for some of that." She bobbed her brows and went onto all fours in front of him.

Gage had to keep from snarling at the sight of all of her curves. And between those lush thighs, she was pink, glistening and ready. "You are so incredibly beautiful." His voice was thick with need. Gage kneeled behind her.

His touch was urgent as he gripped her hips. It couldn't be helped though. "So damned soft," he whispered. With extreme reluctance, he looked up at the canopy above them, focusing his senses for a few moments.

"What is it?" Edith looked back over her shoulder. Her eyes were wide.

"Just double-checking before I'm inside you. I have a feeling I won't be able to concentrate on anything else. I'm sure they're long gone, just wanting to make sure."

"Maybe we should wait or put some distance between ourselves and this place." Concern was etched into her features.

"Yeah we should." He was elated to see a look of disappointment cross her face. "But that's not going to happen." He crouched over her, slipping his hand between her legs. "I'm afraid this first time will need to be quick." He found her clit and began to rub softly. Her mouth opened a little and her eyes glazed over. "I would normally make you come multiple times. Make you come long and hard. I so wish we had the time."

She moaned. "That's okay." She was already panting.

His cock felt thick and ready between his legs. His balls felt tight yet heavy. Gage needed to bring her to the edge because he wasn't going to last. No fucking way. Not with Edith.

He positioned himself between her wet folds and pushed in, just his tip. Gage grit his teeth. So good. So damned good. He pushed in a little more, moving his hips in circular motions. Working at keeping his baser needs in check. Needs like wanting to ram into her. Take her hard and right now. Sweat beaded on his brow. Deeper and deeper, Gage eased in slowly. Edith made mewling noises. He eased off of her clit for a moment, wanting this to last a little longer than two seconds. He'd also promised her he wouldn't come inside her. Right now, he was sorry he'd done that. He wanted his seed inside her. He wanted her swollen with his child. He just wanted her, period, but that was his dick talking. His dick had fallen deeply and madly in love. She felt that good.

What was not to love though? Edith arched her back as he bottomed out inside her. She cried out as his hips hit her ass. Then the animal in him took over. His bear was done waiting. He gripped her hips, loving how her flesh dented by his fingers. This was a real female. One with some meat on her bones. He thrust into her and she yelled. The sound laced with pleasure. He thrust again and again. Watching how her ass jiggled with each hard plunge. She cried out each time his hips hit her ass.

Her mouth was open. Her eyes were wide. Her pussy hugged him, and it hugged him hard. Being inside her was everything he thought it would be. Tight and hot. "Oh hell!" he growled as his groin began to tighten. As everything began to prepare for release. This was going to be tough. He reached around her, finding her swollen nub. Gage didn't waste any time on getting to work. He rubbed on her sweet spot for all he was worth. Not too hard. Easy. Not too fast.

Her channel tightened around him like a vice and she groaned. The sound deep and primal, like it had resonated from between clenched teeth. Her pussy spasmed around him. *Sweet Jesus!* Gage fought for control. It took everything in him not to give in to all of these sensations and just to come inside her.

At long fucking last she began to come down and he slowed, when all he wanted to do was to pound into her. To make her come again while he took what he needed. *No! Fuck!*

It physically hurt him to pull out of her sweet, tight heat.

Edith moaned in protest. She did something unexpected and turned around. Her legs splayed, resting her weight on her elbows. Her gaze was glassy. Her cheeks flushed. She watched in what looked like, fascination as he fisted his cock and began to tug, using hard strokes. All he wanted was to bury himself back into her slick folds. Even her fur was wet. She licked her lips, still panting hard. Her chest heaved. So sexy, so damned perfect. Gage locked eyes with hers. Those beautiful green orbs pulling him in.

The first spurt erupted, landing on her belly, the second was with more force, it splattered all over her glorious chest. *What the fuck was he doing?* Gage closed his other hand over the tip of his cock and finished the job. "I'm sorry," he groaned. "Shit, I'm one sick fuck, Curls," he growled. "But I'd be lying if I said I didn't like the look of you covered in my seed."

"Should I be flattered?" She smiled.

That his bear had enjoyed marking her? That it wanted him to bite her next time as well? That was a resounding yes, he'd never had this happen before, but he couldn't tell her all of that, so he leaned in and kissed her instead. Soft and sweet. Just like her. "Thank you, Curls. Let's get you cleaned up."

She nodded once. "I should thank you right back."

"For messing all over you?' He shook his head.

"Does it make me sick too if I said I didn't mind you coming all over me?"

"Yes, but I happen to think it's a fantastic trait in a female." He kissed her again. A quick press of his lips to hers. Needed to stop doing that. It was a little too lovey-dovey.

Gage worried about heading back into the open during daylight. They should never have had sex. Too damned noisy. What was done was done. He didn't regret it. Not for a moment. "We can't go to the river."

She looked down at herself and then back at him, raising her brows.

"Wait right there." Gage fetched a couple of big, velvety leaves from a nearby plant. "These will have to do." He handed them to her.

"What now?" Edith wiped herself across the chest as she spoke.

He scrubbed a hand over his face. "I'm worried our shelter may have been compromised." He didn't want to put Edith at risk. "I'm inclined to say that we cut our losses, hole up here for the rest of the day and then head out."

She shrugged. "If that's what you think is best."

"You need your clothes though."

"If it's not safe, then I'll survive."

"It's cold at night. The bugs will eat you alive while we travel." He shook his head. "I'll go and fetch your things." There was no other way.

Edith put a hand to her chest. "And if you're captured. What then?"

"Keep going."

"Going where?" She shook her head. "That's not going to work. We go together. We stay together." She narrowed her eyes for a moment and then locked eyes with him. "I know. I'll go."

"No way! No!" His voice held a growl.

She put up a hand. "Hear me out. At least, if I'm caught, you can still get back to the village and get help. I, on the other hand, might end up dying out here on my own."

"If you follow the river you'll eventually make it back to the village. You need to move upstream."

"On my own out here?" She shook her head. "I can't fend for myself or find food. No. I'll go back to camp. I'll fetch my own things. You have to promise you'll head for the village if I'm captured. It has to be this way."

He cupped her cheeks in his hands. He hadn't even realized he had moved. "You're so brave. You know that?"

"I'm just being logical and—"

He kissed her. Gage didn't give a shit about what it meant or what would happen when they finally got back to the village. He kissed the hell out of her. All he cared about was right now. Edith was his friend first and foremost. He was proud of her. He admired her. Most of all, he was afraid for her. "You come back to me, Curls," he murmured as they broke.

"I'll do my level best."

Gage helped her to her feet. It took a minute for her to dress back into her underwear. "I'll take you as close as I can."

Edith nodded, a look of determination on her face. She hopped onto his back and he headed out, taking it slow and easy this time. It took about fifteen minutes and he bent down so that she could slip off. Gage pointed in the direction of their make-shift camp. "It shouldn't take you longer than a couple of minutes," he whispered.

Edith nodded. "Promise me you'll leave if —"

"If nothing. You're coming back. Move quickly and quietly. In and out."

"If I'm not back in five minutes. If you hear anything."

Gage nodded. "Okay. I'll come for you though. Know that I won't stop or give up or…"

Edith smiled. She reached up on her tippy toes, just managing to brush her lips to his. Gage put his arms around her for a second or two before turning her in the direction of the camp.

Five minutes.

Five times sixty seconds.

May as well have been an hour or two. He forced himself to stay still. To stay quiet. To use all of his senses. Just because he couldn't hear, see or smell anything didn't mean it was safe. Not by a long shot. If anything happened to her… anything…

He could still hear Edith moving away. Her footfalls becoming softer and softer. Then, silence. She was gone. Too far away for him to hear her anymore. He felt a moment of panic. Maybe they should have just stuck together. No! She was right. Someone needed to rescue them. All of them. He would bring every shifter, every non-human and take those fuckers down. If they hurt Edith or any of the others, he'd finish them. He stood there for a time, teeth clenched, senses on high alert. Mind wandering to places it had no business going.

His heart beat faster. Was it? Could it be? *Yes!* Footfalls. They were becoming louder. Closer and closer and there she was. Her clothing, as well as the pelt, cradled in her arms. They both moved at the same time. Closed the distance in a couple of frantic strides. He took her into his arms and hugged her close. "Good to see you, Curls." He kissed the top of her head.

"You too." He could hear that she was smiling.

"Let's find a safe place to sleep." He held onto her for a moment longer before letting go.

CHAPTER 15

H er hair was still damp. It dripped down her back and over her shoulders.

Not that she cared.

Not even a little bit.

The world could be ending and she probably wouldn't give a too.

She straddled Gage, her feet on the ground. Her hands clasping his shoulders. His cock deep inside her. Her boobs jerked up and down as he lifted her up and down, as he pounded into her from below in strong, easy strokes.

The sound of their ragged breathing filled the forest. That and the sucking, wet sound her body made with each hard thrust. Edith should be embarrassed about how wet she was. At how close she was to coming, but it felt too good for her to care. If anything, the slapping, sucking noises turned her on even more. If that was even possible. He nipped at one of her nipples, made a growling noise from low down in his throat. So damned sexy. Everything about this man was sexy. From his broad shoulders, to his thick biceps, to that gorgeous smile. The one that made a dimple pop to the left of his mouth. Oh, that mouth. That wicked tongue, those wicked lips. He suckled on her nipple a couple of times before lifting his head. His jaw was tight, his eyes bright. His golden flecks more prominent.

He smiled at her for a half a second before clenching his jaw.

This had all started with him laying her down and sucking on her clit. Sucking. She'd never been sucked before. Licked, yes but sucked, no. It was the best. A soft vacuum over one of the most sensitive places on her body. He hadn't allowed her to come though and had given her the choice of position this time.

Thing was, Edith had ridden this man many times, only, not in the way that she wanted. Not like this. Riding him was superb. It might be her new favorite thing.

Edith moaned. He was big. So very, ridiculously big. He hit every spot inside her. Every. Single. One. She looked down between them, to where they were joined. To where he slid in and out of her. She was about to come. Edith lifted her head; she could feel her eyes rolling back. Could feel her hands clutch at his shoulders. Could feel herself clamp down on him as pleasure rushed through her. Wave after wave. She made a very deep, very weird groaning noise. She had zero control at this stage. Could only feel. Gage held onto her, holding her in place. He kept going. Pushing her higher and higher.

She yelled his name and his lips crushed against hers.

Finally, finally… he slowed, drawing out her pleasure. Easing off. Then he was pulling out, clasping his cock and fisting it. His eyes on hers. Intense and beautiful.

She so wished that he could find completion inside her. She needed to be the one to bring him pleasure. Edith gripped the base of his cock with her own hand. He closed his eyes and groaned, clearly enjoying her touch.

"Let me," she panted out.

"Edith," he groaned, it sounded like both a warning and a plea. She'd ignore the first and go with the second. She scooted back, leaned over and took his dick into her mouth. With her one hand, she stroked his balls and with the other, she fisted the base of his cock. "Oh god, Edith. Shit!" He said a couple more cuss words. His fingers threaded through her hair. "Curls." A deep rasp. Definitely a warning.

She ignored him, deep-throating him. His balls pulled tight in her hand.

"I'm going to. I…" he groaned. His fingers tightened a smidgen on the back of her head as the first spurt hit her throat. She swallowed, continuing to suck him off with her mouth and to pump him with her hand. It took a few more swallows before he was done.

Gage slumped back as she released him. He groaned. His big chest heaved. He lay like that for a time before lifting his head. A beautiful smile played with the edges of his mouth. "That was amazing. *You* are amazing."

She felt her own mouth tug into a smile. Could feel how her cheeks heated. Gage sat up, he put an arm around her middle and pulled her against him, placing a kiss on the top of her head. "What I wouldn't give for a soft bed and a couple of hours to burn."

"Let me guess, you'd sleep like a baby. Don't think I haven't noticed that you don't sleep well out here. That you lie awake keeping watch."

He shrugged. "I don't need much sleep during the summer months. We bears tend to do our sleeping during the winter."

"You hibernate?" She looked up at him.

His eyes were wrinkled at the corners. "I sleep like a human during winter. Six or seven hours at a stretch, may as well be hibernating." He rolled his eyes.

He considered six or seven hours long. Huh! No thank you. Edith needed her beauty sleep. "What, life's too short to spend it all in bed?" She made a face.

"Something like that. Although, if you were in bed with me, I think I'd hibernate winter, spring, summer and fall."

They both laughed. Something clenched in her though. Something deep because there would be no winter or spring for them. There definitely wouldn't be another summer. There was only a couple more days and then it was going to end. She'd somehow managed to convince herself that it was okay when it wasn't. Gage was the kind of guy she could see herself with. At least he had been honest with her and she knew where she stood. There was always the chance that he might change his mind. She somehow doubted it though.

"We'd better get going, Curls." Gage lifted her to her feet.

She forced herself to smile at him. Gage took her hand in his, squeezing it as they set off.

TWO DAYS LATER...

You're sure?" She sounded animated.

"Very sure." His voice was still rough since he had only recently shifted back into his skin. "I recognize that hilly outcrop." He pointed to the right of them.

"Um, okay if you say so." Edith squinted in the general direction. "I can't see a thing. It's still too dark."

"I keep forgetting how blind you are, human," he joked, putting his arm around her shoulders. "If we keep heading west," he gestured to where the sun had just begun to light up the horizon, "we should hit my village in two or three days tops."

"But first we rest." She turned into him, putting her arms around him.

"If that's what you want to call it." He smiled. "I need to scout the area because —"

"No, you need to come to bed with me." She took a step towards their newly made shelter.

Gage narrowed his eyes on hers. He'd like nothing better than to take her up on that very tempting offer. "This part of the forest isn't as dense. It's a little riskier. You make yourself comfortable." He touched the side of her face. "Eat some of those blueberries we found earlier."

Her eyes lit up, then she laughed. It was a beautiful sound. "You know me too well, even after just a few days together. I'm a sucker for delicious food. If you had cupcakes with butter frosting, I'd sing karaoke." She gripped his arm. "I wouldn't recommend it though. I can't hold a tune." She widened her eyes.

"I can think of a couple of things I'd prefer anyway."

He kissed her. "You relax for a few minutes. I won't be long."

"You'd better not be, or I'll be asleep when you get back."

"I can also think of a couple of ways to wake you up." He grinned at her.

She bobbed her eyebrows. "Sounds amazing." Then she gave him a soft push. "Better hurry."

He kissed her again, just a quick touch of the lips. As much as he told himself to stop doing that, he couldn't seem to help it. If she was nearby, he wanted to touch her. Hold her. He wanted to kiss her and hug her and to make love to her. Gage gave a shake of the head. Not make love but fuck. Yep, that's what he'd meant.

He headed out. If he remembered correctly, there was a hollow tree just to the south of there. He'd been on a scouting mission in this part of the woods and had taken shelter in the cavernous trunk before. It was in the direction of the—

Wait. What?

For a moment, it seemed as if the light from the soon to be rising sun had blinked out for a moment. A mere second. Maybe he had blinked. It was possible.

He stood utterly still, turning back to where he had left his female. The hairs on the back of his neck stood up. His heart began to race and his palms became clammy.

There was no reason for him to feel this way. He could have blinked. It might not have been something blocking out the minimal light. What was he saying? He had most likely blinked. It made perfect sense. Only, he hadn't blinked. Gage had always trusted his gut. Right now, despite it still being too dark for those fuckers to be out. It was telling him to run. To save his female. To act! To act now! His gut was screaming it!

Gage didn't wait, he took off in a sprint, changing into his bear form as he ran. Everything became easier, quicker, more fluid.

Her scream punched him in the gut. Right there, dead center. It fueled him. Big fucking time. His hackles went up and a growl was torn from him. The growl only deepened as he entered the clearing where their shelter was.

There she was in a face-off with one of them. It was in man form.

Edith brandished a stick in one of her hands. She had the thing pointed at the beast. His Curls. His sweet, sweet female. She may as well have been holding a toothpick for all her stick would help her. Gage raced forward, putting himself between Edith and the beast. Edith sobbed as she caught sight of him.

"I am one of The Feral," the male said. "Better if you stood down. Go now."

Gage roared, his lips curled back from his teeth. *Fuck you!* He said it in bear, but he was sure that a creature such as this would understand what he was saying.

Fuck you!

He repeated as he walked towards the thing. There was only one of them. For now, at least. More would surely come. He stood a chance against one. At the very least, he could keep it busy long enough for Edith to get away.

Gage heard a cracking noise. It was shifting. Gave him a couple of seconds. He turned to his female and growled. Telling her to go. Willing her to leave.

She shook her head. "You go. We discussed this, remember?" She spoke quickly.

Gage growled again. There was no way in hell he was leaving her. It wasn't happening. That plan had been ridiculous. He never intended on leaving her. Couldn't do it!

If she followed the river like he said, it would be a couple of days tops and she'd be back at the village. Chances were one of the scouting packs would pick up on her scent long before then.

Edith shook her head, her curls bounced. "No, I'm not leaving you."

His sentiments exactly. He turned back, looking into the ugly mug of the griffin. *Bastard!* Those eyes. So cold and calculating.

It made a screeching noise. Telling him to go. A veritable 'fuck off' if he had ever heard one.

He growled low and deep. Telling the griffin in no uncertain terms what it could go and do with itself. He would defend what was his until his last dying breath. He could see by the look in the griffin's eyes that it meant to end him. To injure him gravely at the very least.

"No, Gage!" Edith screamed. "Please."

The griffin came at him. Lightning quick! He could see by the way it traveled that it planned to swipe him with its right talon. He jumped towards the beast as it swiped, using its scaly arm as a vault. Gage aimed at its eye, his paw making sweet contact. His claws gouging at its eyelid. He was sure he punctured deep enough to break through.

Too easy.

It had been too easy. Why hadn't the creature moved away? If anything, its eyes had widened and zoned in on something. Panic had flared in those golden orbs as he struck, hence his success. It wasn't looking at him but past him though. It was looking at…

No.

What?

No.

Gage jumped, turning, doing a one-eighty. *No. God no!* Please let this be some sort of mistake. It was only when he screamed her name that he realized he'd shifted back into his human form. Edith lay in a heap on the ground. She must have run up behind him when that thing struck out with its claw. He'd moved and she'd taken the brunt of the hit. That swipe had been quick and deadly. The creature's claws were sharp. She was gasping for air, bleeding from her nose and mouth. So much damned blood. "You tried to save me, Curls, no! Why would you do that? You should have left or stayed put, not put yourself in harm's way."

Edith smiled. Through all of her pain and suffering, she smiled. "I had to," she managed to get out, between gasps.

The creature made a rumbling noise behind them, but Gage ignored it. He dropped to his knees beside her. He forced himself to calm down. He forced a smile, hoping it was reassuring. "We'll get you back. We'll…"

She shook her head. "No…" There was a look of peace in her eyes. He didn't like it. He hated it. "Don't give up on me, Edith. Don't you dare give up."

"Not. Giving. Up." She gasped and wheezed. "Too late." She kept gasping. Like she couldn't get air in. It was no fucking wonder. *Don't look. Keep your eyes on hers.*

"It's not, no." He was gasping too, only for very different reasons. Struggling to breathe. "I can't lose you."

"Don't blame yourself," she said, her eyes pleading. "My fault."

The creature made another rumbling noise like it was trying to apologize.

"You're going to be okay." He used a firm voice, like if he made her believe it, it might actually happen.

She shook her head. She wasn't gasping as quickly anymore. Her breaths were far more shallow. "Curls, please." His voice broke.

Then he was being shoved aside. Gage flew several feet, landing hard. He felt dazed. It took a second for his vision to clear. Gage needed to move. Had to do it now. He shifted mid-jump, watching in horror as the griffin turned. It had his female up in its talons. The beast rocked back and took to the air. Gage reached up, snagging feathers, but they ripped free. He lost purchase and fell to the ground, landing hard.

Gage roared. Why was it taking her? What the hell could it possibly want with a dying female? He roared again. The sound filled with anguish. With pain. It ended in anger. Bitter and raw. There was a gaping hole in the canopy where the griffin had broken through.

Gage dug his paws into the ground and began to run. He wasn't going to stop until he made it back to his village. He was going to keep his promise to Edith. Gage would amass an army and return to the land of the many towers. He would fight The Feral, taking as many as he could before he himself perished.

CHAPTER 16

THREE DAYS LATER...

G age sat upright. His entire body hurt. Every muscle. Every fiber. Every last inch.

"Easy." Ash laid a hand on his chest and gently pushed him back down. "You need to rest."

Gage frowned. The last he remembered, he was running. He'd been running for a long time... days. His paws had been raw. His throat hadn't fared much better. His flanks kept seizing with cramps, and yet he'd forced himself to carry on. "Edith," he growled. "I have to go." Gage jumped from the bed, crumpling to the floor as pain shot up his legs.

"You're in no state to get up, give it a few more hours," his brother said.

"When did I get here?"

"About three hours ago, so not long enough for you to be getting out of bed already," Ash said. "Don't you remember?"

"No." He shook his head. He planted a hand on the floor to try to get himself up. Gage snarled from the pain that rushed up his arm. His hands were bandaged. His feet too. His muscles felt slow. It felt as if he was bruised all over. "I need to lead a team. Your female, the children. We have to get them back. Those fuckers " His voice was hoarse, he was breathing heavily even though he hadn't done anything. Why was his brother so calm?

"No, we don't." Ash shook his head, his eyes bright. Then he smiled. "They're here."

"What?" Gage frowned.

"Alice and the children. The creatures let them go."

"What? Are you sure?" That couldn't be right. He felt himself frown.

Ash smiled. "Very sure. They were returned yesterday."

It didn't appease Gage. Not in the least. "We still need to go and fight. Stop those fuckers from taking any more of our females. From harming them."

"No one was harmed. Even Meredith was returned."

"What? An unmated female?" Disbelief was etched into every word. "That can't be. It doesn't matter." He raked a hand through his hair. "We still need to go and teach them a lesson. They forced themselves on Meredith."

"No," Ash disagreed, he was frowning heavily. "She wasn't forced to do anything. At least, that is what she has maintained, and I'm inclined to believe her. She said that she was treated fairly."

"No." Gage shook his head. Ash had been misled somehow. "What did they want with Alice, the children?

I'm not buying it. They're evil, Ash, you have to believe me."

"They were curious. Alice said they haven't seen young in many years. They don't have any fertile females left. Apparently, all of their females—"

"I know all of this. They died from clutch sickness…" His patience was growing thin. "I'm not sure what they're playing at. I don't trust them. They have no right abducting innocent females and children just because of what happened to them."

Ash's gaze hardened. "I don't think they went about things the right way, but Alice assures me that they are not a bad bunch. They wanted to see young ones. They were completely captivated by the cubs. They asked a lot of questions about shifters and humans. They want to mate humans of their own. Not our humans though." His voice grew steely. "They want to breed their own young. They were curious, that's all."

Curious his ass. What the fuck was Ash on about? "Where is Callum's female then?" Gage demanded. "Has she been returned too?" Gage could hear the skepticism in his words. This didn't make any sense.

"Yes." Ash nodded. "They were all returned yesterday, unharmed. They wanted to talk to a pregnant human. Especially since she is pregnant with a shifter child. They asked her a whole bunch of questions. They want to take humans as mates. That's all. They have promised to leave us alone."

"I don't get it." Gage scrubbed a hand over his face. "I don't understand."

"I don't think they will be back." Ash poured a glass of water. He popped a straw into the glass and held it out to Gage. "If they try anything again, I will be the first to launch an attack." His jaw tightened.

"And you just believe them? You plan to let them off the hook so easily. They took Alice, Ethan—"

"I know," Ash growled. He quickly schooled his emotions "We need to be logical about this. Would I like to teach them a lesson? Sure. Do I think going up against a formidable foe like the griffins would be an easy task?" He shook his head. "From what Alice has told me, they are strong and there are a lot of them. It would not be a good idea to go against these Feral. It might be suicide. If they leave us be, we'll leave them."

"So, that's it then, we just wait until they come back and take more of—"

Ash's whole stance hardened. His eyes seemed to darken. "If they pull something like that again, I will amass an army. We'll utilize human weapons if we have to. I will bring them down." Ash moved the glass of water back towards Gage.

Despite the burning in his throat, Gage ignored the glass. "What about Edith?" His voice hitched as he said her name. His heart seemed to stop mid-beat. Everything seemed to still. He knew what Ash's answer would be, but he had to ask anyway.

His brother looked grave. "No." He shook his head. "We had hoped that she was with you."

Gage squeezed his eyes shut. His worst fears were realized.

"Where is she?" Ash asked. "I know that the two of you were taken but…"

Gage shook his head. "Edith is dead." He cleared the lump in his throat, swallowing it down. "She was wounded in a battle with one of those fuckers." He growled, wanting to maim, to kill. Wanting to send an army to destroy them. "She got between it and me… tried to protect me or something. I should have known she wouldn't stand by and watch me die. She thought that thing was going to kill me." He shook his head, wishing he had acted differently. If he had known what she planned, he would've taken the knock.

Ash frowned heavily. "Are you sure she's dead?"

"Yes!" Gage spat. He huffed out a breath. "I'm sorry. Yes, I'm very sure, it was a mortal wound, similar to the one I sustained on my chest. I'm not sure how she held on as long as she did." He felt his eyes sting. "She was bleeding… dying…" It came out all choked. "And that fucker took her. There was no way she could have survived."

"I can see you cared for the female."

Gage clenched his teeth. He nodded once.

"I'm sorry." Ash's expression was grave. "I wish I could say something to make you feel better."

"It won't work, so don't bother trying."

Ash came up behind him, he put his arms around Gage and lifted him back onto the bed.

Gage bit back a moan. He was in a bad way.

"Can I bring you something to eat?"

Gage's stomach churned. He shook his head.

"Get some rest," Ash said, "I'll bring something in a few hours, you should be much better by then.

Gage nodded. He turned away, allowing himself to sink into a disturbed sleep.

"You got her killed." Followed by a pause. "Wake up, you bear fuck!"

Gage opened his eyes and turned himself onto his back so that he could look into Jacob's eyes.

"You didn't protect the human." The male's gaze was hard, his hands were curled into fists. It was safe to say that he was pissed.

Gage couldn't deny it. He wished to god that he could, but he couldn't. Gage hadn't done enough to protect Edith. Not nearly enough. In fact, it was safe to say that he had put her in harm's way. Anger rose up in him nonetheless. Who did this pup think that he was? "What is it to you?" he snarled.

"I… I…"

"Spit it out." Why was he goading him like this? What purpose did it serve?

"Not that it's any of your fucking business, but I loved her."

Gage burst out laughing. He had to hold his stomach he was laughing so much. It wasn't lost on him how nuts he sounded. How little humor his fucked up laugh held. He felt a bit off his head right now.

"Stop it!" Jacob pointed at him, his face a mask of rage. "Stop that, right fucking now."

Gage stopped but not because the pup had commanded it. "You spent one night with her months ago. How is it that you loved her?"

Jacob shrugged. "It was more than one night. I saw her after that. She came to see me a good couple of times, but I had to turn her down. Hated to do it. I haven't been able to get her off my mind. I've been with plenty human females, she's the only one I wanted to see again. I was sad when she stopped coming to the Dark Horse and was so happy to see her here last week. I planned on going straight to her on my next leave. Why am I even telling you all of this?" The male suddenly looked tired. His shoulders slumped. "It doesn't matter anymore, does it? You couldn't protect her." Jacob pointed at him. "You fucked up!"

His words hit the spot. They hit in a big bad way because they were true. They were the same words that had been running around in his own head. Over and over. Gage had let Edith down.

"You got her killed," Jacob snarled. His eyes were glowing. "Couldn't even protect her."

That anger was back. Rushing through him. Burning in his veins. "Shut the fuck up!" he snarled.

"I won't! Why don't you make me, asshole?"

The male didn't need to ask twice. Gage rushed him. Weak muscles be damned. Right now, he felt fuck all. That wasn't entirely true. He felt too much. Overloaded with hurt. With pain so consuming.

When his fist connected with Jacob's face, some of his anger subsided. None of the pain did though, that blossomed. "How dare you?" he shouted, watching as Jacob staggered back. It didn't take the male long to get his feet back under him.

Jacob rushed him, knocking him off balance. He pounded a left to his eye and a right to his cheekbone. Pain exploded. He told himself to fight back but any fight he may have had in him left. Poof! Gone. Gage staggered back, landing on his ass.

Hurting Jacob wouldn't change things. It wouldn't bring her back; nothing would. If only he could've done things differently. He should never have had sex with her. He'd allowed his desire to cloud his judgment. To cloud his senses. To get in the way of her protection. Now she was gone.

His fault.

All on him.

Jacob was shoved off of him before another punch could hit home. It was Ward, his muscles were bunched. When he looked behind the wolf Alpha, he saw his brother standing in the doorway, chest heaving. "What the hell are you doing?" he shouted at Jacob.

"Have you lost your mind?" Ward asked the fallen wolf, his voice even.

"This bear couldn't protect Edith. It's his fault she died," Jacob snarled, getting back to his feet. He wiped some blood off his cut lip.

"And you know this how?"

"He's still breathing," Jacob said simply. "He's still fucking breathing, that's how I know."

"He's right," Gage agreed. Edith had asked him not to blame himself. She had known him pretty well, even after just a few days. In all the ways that counted he couldn't help what he was feeling though. He couldn't help that Jacob was right.

"Bull-fucking-shit!" Ash growled. "There was nothing you could have done."

"You weren't there." Gage's eyes pricked. "How would you know?"

"I know you and that's enough. Have you eaten yet?"

Gage snorted. He shook his head. "I'm not hungry." He felt his eye throb. It was probably going to swell some before it healed.

"Listen and listen good." His brother got that steely look of determination. "You are going to get your sorry ass out of bed." Ash narrowed his eyes. "You're showering, dressing and you're eating. It's been two days. You still have those bandages on." His eyes moved to his hands. "You don't even need them anymore. Furthermore, you stink."

Gage didn't say anything.

Ash turned to Ward. "What are you going to do with him?" His brother tossed a dirty look at Jacob.

"You…" Ward paused, he looked like he felt sorry for the male. Gage wanted to break Jacob's nose, but at the same time, he felt sorry for him too. Ward looked down at his feet and then back at Jacob. "I think it would be best if you worked off some of this energy. A male who sits around inside his own head will get himself into trouble." He glanced at Gage before looking back at Jacob.

"Fine." Jacob shook his head. "I'm sorry this happened."

"I think you're apologizing to the wrong person," Ward said.

Jacob turned to Gage. "I'm sorry. I cared about her." His jaw tightened. "I cared a lot."

"I cared about her too." Gage's throat was thick with emotion. "That's why I'll accept your apology."

Ward and Jacob filed out of the room. "You'll do as I asked?" Ash asked him.

Gage nodded. "Yeah."

"Ethan wants to see you. He's been begging. He misses his uncle."

A smidgen of light in the dark. Like a burning match in a vast underground cavern. Gage couldn't help but smile for a moment. It hurt more than just his face. "I would love to see him."

"I'll bring him by later."

Gage nodded. His brother was an asshole. If Ethan was coming, he would be sure to clean up. He had to. Ash knew that he wouldn't want to worry his nephew by looking like shit.

"Good." Ash smiled. "I'll see you later."

CHAPTER 17

H igh slate ceiling. Wooden beams. The room was round and large but she was oh so very comfortable. Very sleepy. In fact, she wanted to close her eyes for a bit more, so she did. Much better! So cozy and warm.

"Human." A high-pitched, distinctly feminine voice.

Edith sighed, not wanting to listen. Sleep was better. She wanted to turn over, to face the other way but something held her in place.

"Human. It is time to wake up." The voice again. Irritating!

Go away! It came out as a garbled mumble.

The woman shook her and she opened her eyes again. Edith turned her head towards the irritating woman. She had to look up and up, even though the lady was sitting on the edge of her bed. Wow, but she was tall… with such smooth, olive skin. Boobs. *Odd.* The woman was topless. She had a short, leather skirt around her waist. It looked soft and tan and reminded her of... of... she looked back up at the woman's face. Those eyes, a beautiful yellow, golden color.

A griffin woman. Was it possible? Must be. The lady smiled. "How are you feeling?"

"Why?" She frowned.

The griffin lady looked at her funny. "You almost died. Don't you remember?" She narrowed her eyes.

"What? No! I almost died? Not possible." And yet she knew it was. Edith sucked in a deep breath. She looked down at her chest. It was tightly bandaged, from under her arms to where her ribs ended. Edith rubbed her hands over the crepe bandages, wincing. Not because she felt any pain but because she expected pain to flare up.

So much pain.

So much blood.

Sure, there had been a few deep lacerations from the griffin's claws, but most of the damage had been on the inside. She'd felt warm and cold. Sweaty and yet at peace. She felt her lungs filling with blood. It had been thick in her throat and on her tongue. So hard to breathe. So hard to stay conscious. "Gage," she cried. "Where is Gage?"

"Cadon saved your life but there was no time for him to explain things to the bear. As it was, you almost didn't make it. He had to use three feathers to bring you back from the brink of death."

Edith had felt her life slipping away. She had spoken with Gage, told him not to blame himself and then, from there, her memory was hazy. "Feathers? I don't understand." A memory stirred inside her mind, but it wasn't strong enough to surface.

"Griffins possess limited magical powers. Those of healing."

Griffins are magical. Gage really was going to have to roast his nuts over a fire. She longed to see him again. Did he know she was here? Did he know she was alive?

The griffin woman went on. "We have limited reserves and so, we must use our powers wisely." Her eyes clouded for a moment. "Our powers are infused in our feathers. The more golden our plumes, the more vibrant our power. Griffins with black feathers have exhausted their reserves."

"Oh!" Edith could hardly believe what she was hearing. "So even though Cadon knew he was using up some of his powers, he still chose to save me?"

"But of course. Cadon is a good male."

"Probably did it so that he can try to mate me." It just slipped out. "Don't get me wrong, I'm grateful, it's just…"

The griffin smiled. "I am sure that was the last thing on his mind. He has been very worried about you."

"Has he really?" Sarcasm dripped from every word.

"Our males can be brash and pig-headed. They were idiots in the way they have gone about things, but I assure you that they would never harm anyone. All of those who were taken have been returned, unharmed."

"That's good news at least but we're talking about them abducting women and children and trying to force themselves on us."

She shook her head, frowning. "Force? No, you must be mistaken. Our males would never force themselves. Like I said, they went about things the wrong way, but their intentions were good. I assure you. Everyone has been very worried about you. Cadon most of all. He is at the base of this tower and refuses to leave."

"You're sure it's not because he wants to try to persuade me to mate with him?"

She folded her hands in her lap. "Quite sure."

"Okay then, I would like to meet Cadon. Would that be possible?"

"Yes." The woman nodded once. "He would like that, but first you must eat and drink. You have been asleep for four days."

Edith's eyes widened. "What? So long?"

The griffin nodded. "We gave you some sleeping herbs to keep you under. The healing process is a painful one… or so I have been told." The woman reached for a bowl of something that smelled absolutely delicious.

Suddenly, Edith was ravenous. She propped up her pillows so that she was in more of a sitting position. Although she felt a bit weak, she was fine otherwise. There was no pain at all. "So, you have never needed to be healed yourself?"

The woman got that same faraway look. Edith would say that she seemed really sad. She shook her head. "The power does not seem to work on our kind, if it did, we would not have lost so many of our females." She brought a spoon of the… it was either thick soup or thin stew… to Edith's lips.

Edith took a mouthful. She chewed a few times and swallowed. It tasted as good as it smelled. "That makes sense. Your men would've healed their mates otherwise."

"Yes, and they tried anyway." The woman brought

another spoonful to her mouth. "Some exhausted all of their powers. They would not give up even though they knew trying was futile."

She swallowed. "That's so sad." Edith could picture it. Maybe she had misjudged the griffins. "What is your name?"

"Davina... and you are Edith." The griffin female smiled, her eyes scrunching at the corners.

"Yes," Edith said, taking another bite. They were silent for the next few spoonfuls. It gave her a chance to study Davina. High cheekbones and full lips. She had chestnut colored, shiny hair. Muscular for a woman, with broad shoulders like a swimmer, or someone who could change shape and fly. Her breasts were small and high. Her legs long and athletically built.

The most feminine things about her were her voice and her hair. Everything else was a touch on the masculine side. It didn't matter because Davina was still beautiful in her own way. One of the last remaining griffin women. She had to be one of the infertile females "Are you mated?"

Davina nodded and smiled. "Yes, Maxum and I have been together for many cycles." She held out another spoonful, but Edith shook her head.

"I'm full, thank you. It would be great if I could have a sip of water." She gestured to the jug of water on the table next to her bed.

Davina poured some into the golden goblet and held it out to her. Edith drank deeply.

"Are you feeling better?" the other woman asked.

"Much." Edith felt more energized after eating. Not nearly as tired as she had been.

"That's good. You will be able to return home soon then. Shall I call Cadon now?" Davina raised her brows.

"Yes, please." Home. Funny how the first thing she thought of was the shifter village and of Gage.

"Just so that you know, Cadon is one of the males who lost his mate to the clutch sickness. Our males mate for life. He does not see you as a potential mate. Cadon is one of those destined to be alone for the rest of his days."

"I didn't realize. How terrible for him. Are there lots of your kind who will have to be alone?"

Davina nodded. "Alas, yes." She cocked her head. "You were not to know. I thought knowing might make you feel more comfortable being around him."

"Thank you." The griffin lady was right.

Davina turned her head and made a high-pitched noise. A large griffin was at the entrance of the tower in a second. The griffin was brown for the most part, some of his feathers were black. His eyes and great beak seemed more golden. He shifted and true as nuts, it was the guy who had ambushed her in the clearing. For a second, she could just stare at him, reminded of that moment when she saw him. Of the fear that had turned her blood to ice.

She'd screamed. A reaction. One she quickly came to regret. Her scream had alerted Gage and instead of following the plan, he'd rushed to save her. It had both warmed and terrified her. Especially because she was convinced she'd have to watch him die. In the end she couldn't simply stand by and do nothing. She had to try to help Gage, and it had turned out to be a terrible mistake. They stood there staring at one another. It seemed as if they were both remembering the events that had led them there.

Davina broke the moment. "I will leave you to talk." She pulled the leather skirt off as she turned, showing off long legs and a really great ass. So athletic. She shifted. Her plumes were a bright golden color. Dazzling. She was smaller than the males of her species. Also, much sleeker built. Davina screeched once and leapt from the ledge.

"I am glad to see that you are in good health." Cadon fastened a loincloth around his middle. "I was told that humans prefer the sexual organs to be covered."

"Yes, that's true, thank you."

"Strange." He paused, fumbling with the tie for a moment. "We still have so much to learn about your species."

"Yeah, you really do." She wasn't going to lie to him.

"I'm glad you asked to see me." He shifted from foot to foot, looking down at the golden floor before locking eyes with her. "I'm so terribly sorry for what happened. Leukos wished to speak with you. He said that you were interesting to talk to, that you had enlightened him about a good number of things. We would never have interfered if we knew you had already mated that bear. Or if we had known you would be hurt."

"So, he thought he'd just abduct me again and at any cost?" She couldn't keep the sneer from her voice.

"I am so sorry I hurt you."

She huffed out a breath. "This isn't going as well as I hoped it would. The reason I called you here was to thank you for saving my life. Yet I find myself getting upset with you at the same time. You were going to hurt my friend."

"I had my orders to bring you in."

"At any cost?"

Cadon shook his head. "No, not at any cost. I waited and watched. I planned to pick you up while the bear was gone. He wasn't supposed to make it back as quickly as he did. Also, the animal shifters are far punier than we had anticipated. One small touch and their bodies tear apart." He shrugged. "The plan was to knock him out, so that I could bring you to my king as instructed. It did not go as planned. I deeply regret almost killing you."

"You guys really can't keep going around abducting people and holding them against their will. You can't go around hurting and almost killing people either." She sighed. "Having said that, I accept your apology. I'm grateful to you for using up some of your powers to save me."

"I would have plucked myself bald to save you." His brow was creased. He had this whole puppy dog look going on.

Edith bit down on her lower lip to stop herself from laughing. Thing was, Cadon was being completely serious. That and completely sincere. It would be rude of her to laugh.

"I deeply regret what happened. My king was most upset. The Feral will no longer abduct females. What happened to you has changed our minds on that note. Believe me."

"What about children? Do you plan on kidnapping more innocent children?" She raised her brows, looking at him pointedly.

"We will no longer abduct anyone. A task team has been assembled to infiltrate a major human settlement."

"Okay." Edith wasn't sure she liked this idea of theirs. "To what end?" She could guess.

"Their mission will be to learn as much as possible about humans. Especially the females of the species. I am one of the chosen few who was selected." He beamed, looking pleased with himself.

"Congrats! I think. I still worry that someone might end up hurt. Most probably one of the humans you come into contact with."

Cadon shook his head. "All of the males who were selected are loners, like me. Males who lost their mates. It is purely a fact-finding mission. We need to learn as much as possible about human females but not with the intention of mounting them."

"So, no serious mingling with the women?"

"No, not in the way you are thinking. You see, we quite literally cannot go down that path. It is impossible."

She couldn't help laughing. "Impossible my ass! You are going to meet and talk with human women. It's not that far-fetched or impossible."

"Those of us who lost mates are dead to other females. It is impossible. We will find out as much information as possible and take it back to those who are trying to find a mate."

"Oh. I see! I'm sorry… I guess."

Cadon bowed his head.

"That sounds like a better plan. I hope that you will take your time?"

"We will mainly observe. Teach what we learn to the males back here at the nesting grounds." He was actually quite a sweet guy. Edith felt sorry for him, could sense his deep sadness and loss.

"I am sure you would like to freshen up and to change." He pointed in the direction of the bathroom. "Soren fashioned some clothing for you out of the pelts."

"That was sweet of him." She looked at the tiny skirt and what looked like a fur skin bikini top. "I think," she added when she actually thought of putting them on and going out in public.

"I will leave you." Cadon bowed his head for a moment. "Call me when you are ready to leave. I will be at the base of the tower."

CHAPTER 18

Her feet touched the ground and Cadon let go. Two silent flaps later and he was touching down next to her. Within a few seconds, he was in his human form, hand clutched over his junk. Maybe these griffins had a chance at making it work with humans after all.

"Good luck with your mission." She held out her hand.

Cadon looked at her outstretched arm and frowned.

"It's a human custom, we shake hands in greeting."

He gently clasped his fingers over hers. Edith shook once and let go. "That's it?" he asked.

"Yes, that's it." She smiled.

"I've already learned something. I am sure that your male will be very happy to see you."

"Nah," she snorted, waving her hand. "He's not mine."

Cadon cocked his head, it was a gesture that reminded her of a bird. All the griffins did it when they were thinking something through. "You may not think of him as yours, but I think that he thinks of you as his."

"You think so?" Hope was a terrible thing. She didn't want to feel it. Gage had been clear but then again, things changed. Didn't they?

"I do think so, yes. The way he defended you, would die for you, told me otherwise."

"He was doing his duty." *Not going there.* Too dangerous to think along those lines.

"Yes, that also makes sense, although," he scrunched his forehead up in thought, "I was quite sure. It is what I observed. It's the little things sometimes, the way one person looks at another, touches another. I guess I was mistaken."

"How long did you watch us?"

"About an hour."

Shew, for a second there…

Cadon touched the side of her arm. "I need to go now," he whispered, almost too softly for her to hear. "All of the best, human." Then he shifted and was gone. As in, the whole thing happened in about three seconds flat. Those griffins sure were fast. She didn't have a chance to ask him to point her in the right direction or tell her how far she was from the village.

She walked around in a circle. Not sure which direction to take. Edith could hear the river. Gage had told her on more than one occasion that if she followed it upstream that she would arrive at the shifter village. That theory was about to be tested.

Or not.

A group of four wolves broke from the forest ahead. They were huge. Far bigger than regular wolves, which told her that they were shifters. She looked for a huge bear with golden eyes, for Gage, but he wasn't amongst them. Her heart sank. It looked like she was in deep. Like it or not. A large grey wolf with dark eyes broke from the group, he sprinted to her while the others continued to lope.

Edith looked down, pulling at the tiny skirt, she may as well be naked. Her clothes had been beyond salvageable and the griffins didn't have actual clothing. At least the skirt was something between a skirt and shorts. More like a tiny skirt and underwear. The top was ridiculous; she was spilling out everywhere. She put a hand across her chest, trying to cover up.

The wolf skidded to a halt, its tongue lolling. Its eyes glinting. There was the cracking noise. First the fur receded, together with the claws and jaw. Then everything seemed to tighten and shorten; primarily it's limbs.

Jacob.

Someone she knew. "Edith," he growled, enveloping her in his arms. "I thought you were dead. Gage told us…" He hugged her tighter. "I'm so glad he was mistaken. I'm so glad to see you."

"You too." She meant it, although, not in the same way he did. Edith could barely breathe.

"Are you okay? Did they hurt you?" He pulled back, looking her over.

"I'm fine. A little underdressed but okay."

"We only just left. The village can't be more than a fifteen-minute lope from here." He gave her another quick hug. "Let me change back into my fur and I'll give you a lift."

"That would be great." It was weird to think that she'd been so in lust with Jacob, but that's all it had been. A crush, an infatuation. Now that she knew what the real thing felt like. At least, something she thought could become real, given time, she felt silly to have ever thought otherwise. Jacob was really nice, but he wasn't hers. He wasn't Gage.

She'd made up her mind, Edith was going to tell Gage what she felt for him. If he turned her down, then so be it. At least she would have tried.

"You have to see this." Ash was out of breath as he rounded the corner, gripping the door jamb as he entered the dining area.

"You told me to eat, and I'm eating," Gage snapped, instantly regretting it. He was acting like an asshole. It wasn't Ash's fault he had fucked up and gotten Edith killed. That was a cross he had to bear all on his own. "I'm—" He was about to apologize when Ash slapped him on the back. Hard. The fork flew from his hand. "The fuck!" he growled.

"Leave it and follow me." Ash was grinning from ear to ear. It was weird, Gage wasn't used to seeing him like this. Maybe on the day he mated Alice. Or on the day his cubs were born. Definitely when he was playing catch with Ethan. Having that thousand-watt smile directed at him though, was disconcerting.

"What?" Gage asked as he followed Ash. "Slow down I'm still rec—"

No.

Not a fuck.

"Edith?" He wasn't sure if he was seeing correctly.

"Edith?" he repeated louder this time. His voice still laced with a good dose of disbelief.

"Gage!" She shouted as she caught sight of him. She pulled away from Jacob. *What?* The male had his arm around her. His hackles rose. What the fuck was Jacob doing touching his female?

No!

Shit!

No! What was he thinking? She wasn't his. His stupid lust-riddled brain had almost got her killed in the first place. He would end up hurting her again if they continued. Not that there was a *they* because there wasn't. Forget about getting her killed; he'd break her heart like he had Savannah's. He was bad news, unable to commit. She wanted kids and a family. She wanted a family home on the lake. Edith deserved all of that. He wasn't even on the goddamned list. It took years to get to the top of that asshole list. In the meanwhile, she'd have to wait. Long distance relationships didn't work for shit. Even when they were between two people who could actually commit. *No! Fuck!* His sweet Curls deserved better.

Then she was throwing herself into his arms. Jacob's scent was all over her. All fucking over. He growled low and deep, his chest rumbling. Everything in him told him to take the male down and then to put his scent back on her and to do a proper job this time.

Edith pulled back, she was frowning heavily. "Is everything okay?"

"Everything is great. I'm shocked to see you." He reached out to touch a lock of her hair but pulled back at the last moment. "I thought… I thought I got you killed,

Curls." His voice dropped low as he fought to control the emotions welling up in him. His nose itched. His eyes stung.

"I told you not to blame yourself," she all but whispered. Her green eyes wide, locked with his. Filled with emotions he'd rather not decipher.

"He did blame himself though," Jacob said as he walked up, standing next to her. "Even I blamed him."

"I knew you would blame yourself." She ignored Jacob. Score to him! Not that it mattered. "And, I told you not to." She was smiling broadly. Looking at him with such expectancy.

"How is it that you survived?" He ran a hand through his hair. "I'm so happy to see that you're okay. I can't believe it."

"Someone had better get a fire going because I was right about the griffins having magical powers."

"No shit! They healed you?"

"Yeah, it's their feathers. They have healing powers." She went on to explain how a male called Cadon had saved her and how the magic worked.

She talked and smiled and talked and smiled some more. Gage didn't want this moment to end. Edith told him all about the griffins' plans. About how some of their males were loners and that she felt sorry for them. Gage still wanted to hunt the fuckers down and kill them. His Curls was sweet though. Sweet as honey. She forgave so easily. He only hoped she could forgive him too.

The moment came sooner than he wanted. Minutes too soon. Days too soon. A whole lifetime too soon.

"So," she rubbed her toes in the dirt, "I was just on my way to go and see Ana. Figured I'd surprise her since she thinks I died, do you want to come along?" She smiled, but her eyes were sad. Those beautiful green orbs were filled with both hope and sorrow. Like she already knew what his answer would be.

"Thanks, Curls." He should really stop calling her that. It wasn't right. "You're back. No thanks to me, but you're back safe and sound. It was our deal remember?" It hurt to say the words.

Her eyes widened for a moment. Like she couldn't quite believe what she had just heard. "Yeah, but…"

"We agreed, Edith." He had to force out her name.

She cleared her throat and seemed to square her shoulders. Her eyes darted to the side for a moment before returning to his. "Of course." She fake laughed. Others might not realize it was fake but he sure as hell did. That was not her real laugh at all. Then she licked her lips. "I had planned on checking in with Ana and then leaving anyways." She shrugged like it was no biggie. "It's Saturday, right?"

No one answered her.

"Right, Jacob?" She shoulder-tapped him.

"Yep, it sure is." He smiled at Edith.

"Exactly. I have a show day tomorrow. A house I'm definitely going to sell. I have a job to do. A life to get back to." She looked him straight in the eyes as she said it. Good for her. One part of him felt good that she was going to be fine while another part fucking died inside. "You said you would give me a ride back to Sweetwater." She turned to Jacob, pretty much cutting him off from the conversation.

"Sure, no problem." Jacob nodded and then nodded some more, reminding Gage of a lovesick puppy. Little ass-wipe obviously didn't have a clue he was second choice! That wasn't fair to Jacob. He couldn't think like that.

The male grinned at Edith. Again, he was tempted to step in and… *No!* This was for the best. It was!

"Great." She clapped her hands. "You can come with me to Ana's then." She completely ignored Gage.

What else did he expect? He'd hurt her. It was better this way though. He may have hurt her, but she'd be okay. She'd get over it. Jacob would see to that. "Glad you're okay." He turned and walked away before he was tempted to do something stupid.

"What the fuck is wrong with you?" Ash stepped in next to him. He spoke through clenched teeth.

"Leave me alone." Gage shrugged out of Ash's clasp.

"No can do, asshole," Ash growled beneath his breath. "I was once so in lust with a female that I ignored what was right so that I could have her. I knew you were falling for Savannah. I knew you were making a mistake when you pushed her away. That you would regret it."

Gage picked up the pace. "I really don't feel like having this conversation again. Enough already!"

"Oh, we're going to have this conversation whether you like it or fucking not."

"Not." Gage kept walking. He walked right past his house, trying to escape his annoying as fuck brother. "I dumped Savannah because I was no good for her." Truth. He did care for her and, as it turned out, he did love her, even though he had convinced himself otherwise. It didn't stop him from getting itchy feet though. It was how he rolled.

"And that's why you just walked away from Edith?

Because you've somehow convinced yourself that you're no good for her?" Ash asked, eyes narrowed.

"Exactly." Gage pulled in a deep breath. "Only a matter of time before I leave her, so may as well do it now. I guess I'm not much of a shifter in that sense. I can't mate her. I don't want to hurt her," he added the last more to himself.

"I think you're afraid."

"Afraid of hurting her?" Gage snarled, coming to a stop so that he could face his brother. "Hell yes!"

Ash's whole stance softened. "I think you're afraid that she'll hurt you. She's not Savannah."

"I know that... fuck!"

"It was Savannah who had a problem with commitment. She wasn't able to commit fully to just one of us. It screwed with your head."

"Bull!" The word didn't hold much conviction.

Ash made a growling noise and pursed his lips for a moment. "Hell, it screwed with me just as much. Bottom line, Savannah wanted both of us right from the start, and you knew it. You fell for her long and hard and blindly, and when you realized she still had her sights on me, you dumped her just as hard and fast. Then you jumbled things up in your mind so that you could live with it."

"Edith isn't like that," he murmured. "Not that Savannah was a bad person. She was just," he mussed his hair, squeezed the back of his neck, "she was torn."

"Savannah was who she was. A free spirit who happened to fall in love with two brothers." Ash shrugged. "It was a hot fucking mess."

"Yep, it sure was."

"Tell me about Edith," Ash said.

He couldn't help the smile that broke free. It didn't last though; it died a quick-ass death when he remembered that he and Edith were over. That they had never been in the first place. "Edith is amazing. Aside from being so damned beautiful, she's kind and sweet." He shook his head. "How do I risk hurting her?"

"I hate to break it to you." Ash clasped him around the shoulder and gave a squeeze. He let go. "Relationships are full of risks. It's how it works. It's why being in one is so amazing. Each day is like a gift that you give to one another. I'm willing to bet you that Edith would rather have one hundred days, a thousand days, than none at all."

"That's not how it works at all. It's all or nothing." Gage believed in that wholeheartedly. It's how he'd made himself stay far away from Savannah after she and his brother got together.

"You don't have commitment issues. You don't! You need to trust yourself more. Take it slow if you have to." Ash narrowed his eyes. "You do realize that you just handed your female over to Jacob. You put her on a shiny fucking platter and handed her over. Not very smart, bro. Not smart at all."

"I'm not on that list." Anger rolled through him. "She deserves more than one night a month. I can't do that to her."

"Did you ever think to ask if she was okay with it?"

Irritation rushed through him. "Did you not hear the part about her being sweet?" He threw the words at Ash. "I decided for her because she'll agree to the long-distance thing and that's not fair."

"You do know that females like making their own decisions about things, right? That they're quite capable of taking all the facts and—"

"Yes, fuck yes! I want her to be happy though. I'm doing this for her."

"Spare me the bleeding-heart shit! You're afraid, and you're taking the cowardly route."

"You're full of shit," Gage snarled.

"Me?" Ash tapped his chest and grinned. "That's rich." He widened his eyes. "If you gave her the opportunity to choose, I have a feeling she'd choose to be with you. That you make her happy. I'm not sure why – you're a bit of an asshole – and yet I know she'd choose to be with you, no matter what. I know a smitten female when I see one."

Gage ran a hand through his hair. "What if I get cold feet? It's what I do. It's how I roll."

"We already went over this. Your relationship with Edith is different to the one you had with Savannah. Edith is a completely different person. You made a mistake once, all I'm saying is don't make the same one again." Ash blew out a breath through his nose. "You kicked my ass when I couldn't see what was right in front of me. That I was head over fucking heels in love with Alice. I'm returning the favor. I think you're far gone. I'm saying it like it is." His brother put up his hands.

Gage clenched his jaw. He didn't say anything. His mind raced.

"Also, just so you know," he pushed a breath out through his nose, "the list is about to be scrapped."

"What?" Gage couldn't quite believe what he was hearing.

"It's about to be scrapped. The whole list concept is ridiculous. It's stupid. I was against the thing from the start. It's not working. It's not how love goes. You can't tell people when they can and can't fall in love. It sometimes just happens, and usually when you least expect it." Ash tapped him on the back. "It just happens, whether you want it to or not. You've been bit, bro. I suggest you do something about it."

"Before she heads off into the sunset with Jacob." He clenched his jaw.

"Edith doesn't want Jacob, she wants you. Only has eyes for you."

"You think so?" He hated that spark of doubt. He'd once been confident almost to the point of arrogance. Savannah had not only knocked him down a few rungs; she'd knocked him flat on his ass. It was clear that he still had to pick himself up a whole lot more.

"I know so. You need to hurry and do something about it quick, because every second you wait, you'll have to grovel that much longer. She'll be upset and then she's going to get mad."

Gage couldn't picture Edith mad. He hated to picture her upset. It pissed him off, especially since he was the one to have hurt her.

They began to walk in the direction of Ana's house. Her heart was beating so hard she was sure her ribs would bruise. No, that's where she had it wrong, her ribs would be just fine. Her heart on the other hand...

So much for that. She said she would try, and she'd tried. Fat lot of good that had done because she'd failed. But at least she could say that she had tried. Gage, however…

She forced the anger down. He'd never promised more. Although, that wasn't entirely true. He may not have verbally promised her more, but he had promised her more in other ways. Ways that counted more than words. It was like Cadon had said. He'd promised her more in the way he had touched her, the way he had looked at her. Even that stupid nickname had been a promise of sorts. Curls. The way he had said it had warmed her from the inside out. Had he not noticed how she lit up every time he said it? How she had lit up every time she looked at him?

Why had she let herself fall for him? It had all happened so fast. How was that even possible? She was an idiot. Bottom line!

Jacob touched the side of her arm. "Are you okay?" He sounded concerned.

She glanced his way. "Yeah, why?"

He smiled. There wasn't nearly as much happiness in the smile as there had been earlier. If anything, there was hesitancy and uncertainty written there. It made her feel worse.

He stopped walking. "Because you're grinding your teeth."

"Oh." She smiled. It wasn't fair. Jacob was a good guy and she was using him to get back at Gage. "We need to talk." She squeezed her eyes shut for a moment. "I'm sorry, I—"

"You're not into me," he blurted. "I kind of figured."

"It's not that there's anything wrong with you. You're such a good guy. I find myself wishing I…"

Jacob grasped her arms and leaned in a little, looking

her in the eyes. "I know you're in love with Gage."

Oh shit! She felt her eyes fill with tears. "Is it that obvious?"

Jacob nodded. "If you have half a brain then, yes, you'd notice."

She breathed in through her nose trying hard to hold back those asshole tears. "I kind of wish I wasn't but…" She shrugged.

"Maybe he doesn't know. Guys can be stupid like that. Maybe…"

She shook her head. "I think he knows. I don't understand why he's pushing me away. Maybe it's one-sided. Maybe I imagined his feelings for me."

Jacob made a strange noise and pinched the bridge of his nose. "I want to lie right now because I want you for myself, Edith. I want to be the one to swoop in and heal your broken heart. Thing is though, I really *do* think Gage has feelings for you."

"Why is he pushing me away then? I don't understand."

"You'll have to ask him."

The thought terrified her. She'd put herself out on a limb and had been shot down. Edith had gotten the message loud and clear. "No. If Gage decides to take his head out of his ass then… maybe, but otherwise." She shook her head. "I'm going to say goodbye to Ana and then I'm heading home. Will you take me to her, please?"

Jacob smiled at her. It was so warm, so sweet. "I hope things work out, but if you ever decide that you're over that asshole, and you'd like to give a wolf a chance, you'll look me up?"

It was so sweet. Exactly what she had been looking for

from Gage. It ripped her heart open all over again because it reminded her of all she was losing. Make that, of everything Gage had chosen to throw away. "Shit," she mumbled as the tears began to fall. "I'm sorry," she managed to push out through the slew of hot tears.

Jacob pulled her into his arms and held her tight. "I can also be a really good friend," he finally said when her tears began to subside. "No strings attached. I swear."

Edith choked out a teary laugh. "That's good to know." She pulled away and wiped her face. "Thank you."

Jacob cupped her cheeks. "You need to know that you are amazing. One in a million. You deserve to be loved and cherished. You deserve the best." He let her go, brushing some hair off her face.

"I appreciate that."

He rolled his eyes. "I mean it. Wholeheartedly. I find myself wishing I had ignored all the rules and…"

"Don't even say it." She shook her head. "Things happen and don't for a reason. You'll find the right person, Jacob. You know that, don't you?"

He shrugged. "We'll see." Jacob pushed his hands into his jeans pockets. "I'm not really looking."

She laughed. "Trust me, that's the best time, although, it doesn't always go the way you planned." They picked up the walk again. "Good thing I happen to know that Ana has double chocolate ice-cream. A whole tub."

"What does ice-cream have to do with anything?" He made a face.

"Ice-cream somehow has the ability to make you feel better when you eat it." She smiled.

"It does?" Jacob looked skeptical.

"Yep, but it has to be straight out of the tub and shared with friends. You should join us and have a try."

Jacob frowned. "I'll have to take your word for it, but I'm game." He still looked skeptical.

Edith couldn't blame him. Most times, ice-cream really worked. It could magically heal the soul; only, she got the feeling that this time would be different. This time, she would need a lot more than her favorite ice cream to heal her soul.

CHAPTER 19

Was his brother right?

Had he known that Savannah had the hots for Ash when he dumped her? Had he pushed her away for those reasons and not because he couldn't commit? Did his commitment issues stem from what happened in the past? Quite possible. Likely. Or ridiculous?

It didn't matter. All that stuff Ash had said about risk made sense. He needed to put it all out there and then let Edith decide.

Gage rounded the corner. He could see the two of them up ahead. Jacob and Edith. Jacob was hugging Edith. Held her close, one hand rubbing up and down her back, the other threaded in her hair.

He bit back a growl. Green was not a good color on him. It was his own damned fault and it didn't mean anything.

He kept walking, neither of them noticed him. Then

again, he was still a good distance away. Edith wiped a hand across her face as she pulled away. Had she been crying?

Probably.

He was a bastard.

Such a fuck up!

When Jacob cupped her cheeks, he came to an abrupt halt. Gage's heart beat so hard, he was sure it might snap a rib. He wanted to charge them head on and take Jacob out. Friends didn't touch friends in that way. *Fuck that!* He was close enough to hear what the asshole-pup was saying. "You need to know that you are amazing. One in a million." The male paused. "You deserve to be loved and cherished."

It was true.

So true it hurt.

"I appreciate that." Her voice was a soft murmur. Edith didn't pull away. Just stared into his eyes. She said something else that he didn't register.

Gage had seen enough. "I mean it wholeheartedly," he heard Jacob say as Gage turned and high-tailed it the fuck out of there. He'd been there, done that and had the bloody t-shirt and war wounds to prove it. Not again!

If Edith wanted Jacob, she could have him. He wasn't going to be part of it. *Fuck that!*

ONE WEEK LATER...

There was something that could be said about weariness. Absolute and utter bone shattering tiredness. It crept up on you, day by day. It settled in your limbs, weighing you down. Grabbing at you, every part of you. Holding on like it was never going to let go.

That's how he'd woken up this morning. So tired he wanted to pull the covers over his head and never get out of bed. It was a good thing he had a play date with a certain young cub, and so he'd forced himself to get up, to get dressed and to turn up with a smile on his face, whether he felt like it or not.

"Ready?" Gage asked.

Ethan nodded, his eyes bright and wide. Gage pulled back his arm and threw the ball. Ethan caught it, dead-center in his mitt. "This is getting too easy for you," Gage yelled at his nephew.

Ethan threw it back, his throw wasn't as strong, so Gage had to run forward to catch it.

"Let's make this a little more difficult. Are you ready?"

"Yes!" Ethan yelled, punching his mitt a few times.

"Good." Gage loosed the ball, aiming just to the right of where Ethan was standing.

The little tyke caught it like it was nothing and threw out a giggle. One he felt in the gut. He loved this child with all of his heart. Gage had found himself wishing that the boy was his on more than one occasion.

Ethan threw the ball back. "Again, Uncle Gage. Again, again!" He jumped up and down.

"Okay." Gage threw slightly wide a second time, to the left this time.

Ethan caught the ball with one hand, laughing all the while. The little guy was growing up.

"No." Gage feigned shock. "When did you get so good at this?"

"I've been prac… prac… pra-ciss-ing."

Gage bit back a grin. "You've been practicing, huh?"

Ethan nodded in an exaggerated way, as only a four-year-old could. "With daddy."

"Well, I can tell." Gage nodded once.

Ethan beamed.

"How about we take a little break and have a snack?" He mussed Ethan's hair and his nephew giggled.

"Yes, please." He clapped his hands.

They went and sat on the grass. "Let's see what fun stuff your mom packed for us." Gage opened a backpack and pulled out a couple of juice packs, handing one to Ethan. Then he pulled out some sandwiches wrapped in grease-proof paper. "Ham and cheese?" He raised his brow. "One with mustard and one without. I'm guessing you're the mustard fan." He tickled Ethan, who squeezed his juice box, spraying some of the contents all over Gage's shirt. "Hey!" Gage pretended to be angry.

Ethan laughed and laughed. It came from somewhere deep in his belly. Gage couldn't help but join in.

"I don't eat mustard," Ethan announced when he finally calmed down enough to talk.

"You don't? Oh well then, this one's for you." He handed the sandwich without the mustard to Ethan.

They sat in silence for a few minutes, enjoying the food. Then Ethan turned and looked at him, a serious expression on his face. "Why are you so sad, Uncle Gage?"

"Who, me?" Gage shook his head, he even smiled. "I'm not sad." He didn't like the worried look in Ethan's eyes. The kid was too young to feel those kinds of emotions. Especially where he was concerned.

"Yeah, you are." Ethan looked at him some more, this time he really looked at him. "Even though you're laughing and smiling, you're still very sad inside. I can tell."

From the mouths of babes. "I'm just working through some things. It's not a big deal."

"I don't like it when you're sad." Ethan shook his little head, scrunching up his nose.

"I'm going to be fine." He mussed Ethan's hair again, but the little boy didn't react this time, his whole expression still serious. "Sometimes people get sad." Gage shrugged. "They can't help it. I guess I am a bit sad right now, but I'll get better."

"Will you take medicine? Humans take medicine when they are sick. Mommy told me all about it. She's a human," he added, just in case Gage wasn't aware. It was so damned cute.

Gage chuckled. "Medicine doesn't work for being sad. You see, it's my heart that's not feeling so well."

"Your heart?" Ethan's eyes were wide. Then he nodded as if he fully understood. "What about a Band-Aid? If I hurt myself, Mommy puts a Band-Aid on and kisses me better. You should put one on your heart." He rubbed his chin, looking like a four-year-old professor. "I also think you need someone to kiss you better, Uncle Gage." Ethan looked up at him with such innocence.

"It's not as simple as that, buddy." *If only.* He'd fucked up so badly.

"Yes, it is." Ethan nodded, so sincere it was scary, but only because the little guy was right. "One kiss and you'll be all better."

Gage didn't doubt it. "Maybe you're right, buddy." He hugged the little boy. "You're a clever sausage; you know that?"

"I'm not a sausage."

Gage laughed. For the first time in days, it felt real. He felt lighter.

CHAPTER 20

E dith was selling this house today. She could feel it. Her luck was about to change. Although this new potential client had insisted on texting her instead of having an actual conversation, he seemed really keen. Wanted to buy the house for his girlfriend. He even said that he loved the charm of the place.

Lucky girl.

Despite this house being amazing, with views to match, the show day had been a disaster. She'd been there, handing out flyers, only her mind had been somewhere else. Her heart was still back in that shifter village with a guy who didn't deserve it.

If only she could just shut her feelings for Gage off. If only. She would and in a heartbeat. Gage didn't deserve her. *Enough!* She'd wasted enough energy on him already. Back to the job at hand. This house and her life, dammit!

Edith needed to get this place ready for the viewing.

There was only one problem with this property, the owners had already moved out. It was more difficult to sell an empty home. Most people didn't have vision. That, and it was easier to see the flaws, especially on a more dated property. A hint of peeling wallpaper, a broken plug point. A chipped window. It was all laid bare like her stupid, stupid heart. The one she had put on her sleeve. The one she had handed to Gage.

Asshole.

She flung open another window. The place would be nice and airy by the time Mister Carnivore arrived. What a surname. Poor dude must have been seriously mocked at school with a name like that. It didn't matter what his name was, she was going to sell him this house. Lucky bugger. It was an amazing house. He and his girlfriend would be really happy here. So happy. They might even tie the knot on the lawn that led to the lake. Maybe they would say their vows on the jetty. Her heart felt like acting up. Her mind wanted to wander to thoughts of… No… she wouldn't allow it.

Head in the game, Edith made her way back to her car, carefully taking out the vase of flowers. All in bright, bold colors. Long-stemmed roses, irises, and lilies. She planned on placing them on the center island of the kitchen to give the area a warm, family feel. The front door was still open, just like she'd left it. Her arms were full of vases and flowers. The latter distorting her view somewhat. She should've had them make up something a bit smaller. More manageable for someone who was only five foot nothing. Edith walked carefully up the path and took her time negotiating the steps leading to the front door, which she kicked closed behind her. Edith walked straight into an obstruction and screamed because it wasn't an obstruction but a person. The guy was big and all dressed in black. At least, from what she could see of him through all the flowers.

Intruder alert!

Edith did what any woman in her right mind would do and whacked him upside the head with the vase. Flowers be damned.

The vase cracked. Flowers went flying. Water sprayed, landing on the porcelain-tiled floor with a splatter. The intruder crashed against the wall with a groan. Music to her ears.

"Gage?" Her voice was laced with confusion because boy oh boy was she big time confused. "What are you doing here?"

He rubbed the side of his head. "Ow! I forgot how hard you can hit, Curls." Gage smiled at her. Her heart beat faster. Her whole body felt warm and happy. Very bloody happy that he was there. Good thing her mind had better ideas. More logical ideas. *Screw him!*

"You deserved it. I've told you how many times not to sneak up on me?" She plonked the cracked vase down so hard it broke in two, the rest of the flowers spilling out. "What are you doing here? I have a client," she looked at her watch, "arriving in the next ten minutes."

"I had a chat with my four-year-old nephew," Gage said. "He gave me some damned good advice. Ash and I also had a talk, but his advice was convoluted and quite frankly, a little long-winded. It took a four-year-old to put things nicely into perspective for me."

"I'm not sure I follow you." Edith pushed out a heavy breath. Not sure she wanted to listen to what he had to say. "I'm not sure why you're here." She couldn't think of a single reason aside from sex, but that was not going to happen. Not in a million freaking years.

"The four-year-old is my nephew, Ethan." Gage's eyes lit up. "He's such a great kid and smart too. Intuitive. He knew that I've been feeling down. Knew I was sad inside… his words. True though."

Edith swallowed hard, not sure if she wanted to hear more, yet unable to tell him to shut up. It looked like he planned on pulling a one-eighty on her. "Look I'm not sure…" A half-hearted attempt to get him to stop. "You made up your mind." She shrugged.

"Don't you want to hear his great advice?" Gage became animated. She'd missed his beautiful brown eyes. His easy smile.

Edith rolled her eyes. "You've come this far, so you may as well tell me. I doubt it will make much difference." She folded her arms, looking up at him, trying hard to keep her expression neutral. Just because he was here did not mean that this would end up going somewhere. Gage had hurt her.

"Ethan told me I needed a Band-Aid." Gage gave her this amazing half-smile. "A Band-Aid. Have you ever heard anything so logical in all your life? Well, I haven't. The thing is…" He reached out and touched the side of her arm, his eyes filling with… tenderness. "*You* are my Band-Aid, Curls."

Oh shit! That was sweet. So darned sweet. It wasn't enough though. Gage could be sweet and charming. He'd still hurt her though. He could still change his mind. There was no way she could trust him again. Her heart wasn't on her sleeve anymore. It was safely tucked away.

"I know I hurt you."

Big time.

More tenderness appeared in his eyes. Those golden flecks seemed to become more prominent. "I'd like to think that I can be your Band-Aid too. If you'll let me?"

"You can't just come waltzing in here – scaring me half to death in the process – and expect me to forgive and forget. You *did* hurt me. I know you never promised anything but still… I guess I was stupid enough to think that we had something going on, but you pushed me away. You can't suddenly change your mind and all will be forgiven. That's not how it works."

"We did have something. Something real and true and it scared the living shit out of me."

"You should not have thrown that something away then." She pulled her lips into her mouth.

"No," he shook his head, "I shouldn't have. I let my fear get the better of me."

"What is there to be afraid of?"

Gage sighed, he raked a hand through his hair. "I thought I had commitment issues. I didn't want to end up hurting you, Curls. I figured if we ended it now before we became too invested, before *you* became too invested, that I was doing you a favor, but it isn't true."

"That's crazy reasoning." She widened her eyes.

"I know." His jaw tensed.

"It's cowardly too," she spoke softly.

"Yes, it is. I can't deny that. I guess I needed to think things through. I've been miserable without you. I had somehow convinced myself that leaving you was for the best. That we were better off, but I was wrong." His

Adam's apple bobbed. "I wanted to talk to you on that day when we got back after I pushed you away, but you were with Jacob. I saw you guys together."

Edith narrowed her eyes. "What? You thought Jacob and me… that…" She made a groaning noise. Anger and frustration ate at her. "You just assumed the worst of me?"

Gage shook his head. "I didn't. I knew that the two of you were over."

"We were over months ago. I told you that."

"I made excuses though. I was… *still* am afraid. I fell in love with someone once. She happened to be in love with my brother."

"Oh." This was not what she expected. Not even close.

"It turned out that she was in love with both of us. He was the one who ended up mating her. Her name was Savannah, she was Ethan's mom. My nephew, Ethan, the smart four-year-old. Anyway, Savannah died a couple of years back. It was a mess. A complete disaster. Being part of a love triangle is not fun. I didn't so much as lay a finger on her after Ash mated her, but it was like invisible ropes still tied me to her."

"A love triangle? That's not what this is!" she yelled, couldn't help it because he was so far off base. "I'm sorry that happened to you but there is nothing between Jacob and me. Is that what you're afraid of?"

"I know there's nothing between you and Jacob, but I hope it explains some of my apprehensions. The whole thing with Savannah nearly ruined my relationship with my twin brother. We were so close before. Breaking up with Savannah was one of the hardest things I've ever done. It nearly broke me to watch the two of them together, day in and day out. In many ways, what I had with Savannah was young love. It was first love stuff and it still hurt me so bad. I have a feeling we could have so much more, but that would mean taking a serious risk. Taking a leap of faith." Gage took both her hands in his. "I know I pushed you away when I should have pulled. I was stupid and blind and scared. Truth is, I still am but I want this more than anything. I'm lost without you, Curls."

Edith licked her lips, wanting so badly to jump into his arms.

"I know I hurt you. I wish I could take it back, but I can't. Give us a chance. Take a leap of faith with me. I'm falling desperately and totally in love with you, that's why I'm so afraid. What I'm trying to say is, let me be your Band-Aid." He cupped her cheeks and she let him.

Her heart was beating wildly in her chest. "I'm afraid," she said, wanting so much to trust him. "I don't know if…" She wanted to jump into his arms and throw caution to the wind. "I just don't know."

"I do." He smiled, letting her go so that he could tug on a strand of her hair. "I see you left your hair the way I like it."

Edith tried to smooth the riot of unruly curls. No such luck. She shook her head. "I didn't have time to straighten it this morning."

"Bullshit, Curls. You haven't straightened it once since you came back."

She felt her eyes flare wide. "Have you been spying on me?"

"I knew it." He moved in a little closer, not actually touching her. "You haven't given up on me… on us.

Please, Curls."

His eyes. His smile. Him. "Please don't hurt me," she whispered.

"I won't." He cupped her cheeks again; his hands were warm on her skin. "Hurting you would be hurting myself. One and the same."

"I never expected this to happen. That you would be here. That…" She forced herself to stop blabbing. "I'm falling for you too," she all but whispered.

"Thank god!" He put his forehead against hers for a second. "You have no idea how happy I am to hear that." Gage pulled back, looking deep into her eyes. "So, you agree to give us a chance?"

Edith bit down on her lower lip and nodded. "Yes, I do. I don't have a choice because I'm miserable without you."

"This is the part where I kiss you all better." He clasped her cheeks firmer.

Edith smiled. "And I get to kiss you all better as well." She looked at his lips. *Oh, what a mouth.*

"I sure hope so." He moved in, his lips hovering just shy of hers.

Oh shit! "Wait." Her eyes flew open and she pulled back.

"What is it?"

"My client will be here any second. This place is a mess." She lowered her voice. "We can't be kissing each other better in case he arrives."

Gage laughed. "Mister Carnivore?"

"Yes, Mister Carnivore… he's due to…" *What?* Wait just a minute. "How do you know his name?" She could guess. *The little shit.*

"With a name like that, I thought you would have guessed." Gage looked sheepish. "You put me on the spot when you asked for my name, I made one up and sent it. In hindsight the name was stupid." He chuckled. "I thought you would've put two and two together."

Edith had to laugh. "Well, I didn't. This means I don't have an actual viewing. I thought Mister Carnivore seemed really nice. I thought it was sweet that he wanted to buy his girlfriend this house. He told me he loved its charm and that he hoped they'd be happy here for many years."

"I do." Soft and timid.

"What?" She must have heard wrong. That, or she had this all wrong.

"I'm not on that list. I'm not technically allowed to date. They're probably scrapping the whole list thing long-term but I'm not sure when, or what the new arrangement would be. I want to buy this house for us." He shrugged. "I want you and me to work. I want it more than anything. I'm going to move here and when you're ready, you can move in with me. I'm hoping you'll agree to eventually move to the village with me. Especially if we're going to have kids. Shifter young would be safer — "

"Wow. This is suddenly moving fast. You're giving me whiplash here."

"I'm trying to show you how serious I am. I don't believe in long distance relationships. I'm sure we would make it work but it's not what I want for us. I'm moving to Sweetwater and then we'll figure it out."

Gage, kids, him moving here. It all sounded fantastic.

It made her a bit nervous too. "Okay. I want you to move to Sweetwater. You know I love this house." She walked in a small circle, ending with him in front of her. Jeans and a tight tee. "I don't want a long-distance relationship, but we need to take things slow."

"That's why I'm buying this house instead of throwing you over my shoulder. You do know that every instinct is making me want to do the latter?"

"Oh really?" She swallowed thickly, her body doing its own thing again. Good thing she was fully onboard this time.

Gage's nostrils flared. "About that kiss…"

"Yes, about that kiss."

He closed the distance between them and crushed his lips to hers. Edith could barely think coherently when he finally came up for air.

"I think you need to show me every room in this house." Gage was breathing heavily.

"Every room?" She quirked an eyebrow.

"We can start with the main bedroom and work our way through the rest of the house." He bobbed his brows.

"I must warn you, there's no bed."

Gage's eyes seemed to darken. "Since when do we need a bed, Curls?"

Edith laughed. "You're so right."

CHAPTER 21

SIX WEEKS LATER...

"Honey, I'm home." Edith used her elbow to close the door. "I come bearing gifts." Edith rounded the corner and had to stop in her tracks.

Wowza.

Hubba Hubba.

Her mouth went dry and her heart sped up a whole hell of a lot. Gage was about halfway up the ladder wearing just a pair of faded blue jeans and nothing else. Not only that, he was painting the wall, using long even strokes with the roller. Watching him work these last few weeks had been like watching porn. It got her going every time. His muscles popped and his jeans rode low on his hips.

"Are you checking me out?" He glanced over his shoulder, his face lighting up with a smile.

"Maybe." She smiled back.

"We're nearly done with the renovations. I reckon another day or two should do it." Gage stepped down off the ladder, putting the roller onto the tray, placing both on the floor. He wiped his hands on his jeans as he walked towards her. There was a smudge of paint on one of his cheeks and another on his chest, just above his left pec. "Have you given any thought to my suggestion." Gage took the pizza boxes out of her hands and placed them on the nearby table.

"Moving in you mean?"

Gage nodded. "Yeah, moving in. We may as well live together since we either sleep here or back at your place anyway."

There hadn't been a single night they hadn't spent together since he had put a Band-Aid on her heart and had kissed her all better. As in, kissed every inch of her body until she couldn't remember her own name, let alone why she was mad at him.

Edith pulled her bottom lip between her teeth and gently bit down on it, looking up at him through her lashes. "I'm still thinking about it." Of course she was moving in. They'd been furniture shopping together. Had picked everything out for the house. They had their whole future ahead of them. There was no way she was sleeping anywhere but in the arms of the shifter of her dreams.

"So," he pulled her into said arms and kissed her, his hands sliding down to cup her ass, which he squeezed, ending the kiss with a low rumble, "that means I haven't convinced you that moving in with me would be a fantastic idea." His lips were a breath away from hers.

Biting back a giggle she nodded. "I guess not."

"I haven't worked hard enough."

"I guess not."

"Haven't pleased you nearly enough." He buried his head into her neck and kissed her on her pulse.

She giggled and shrugged. "Nope."

"I see you're wearing one of your fancy business suits." He pulled back and gave her the once-over. "Wouldn't want to get any paint or dirt on you. We might need to take this off." He touched the lapel of her jacket.

Edith nodded. "You might be right." She allowed him to peel her jacket off. His big hands cupped her boobs and then her ass. His breathing becoming more labored with every second. Edith loved that she had this kind of effect on him. He pulled the zipper on her skirt down and pulled that off too, his touch becoming quicker, firmer, more urgent.

Edith quickly unbuttoned her blouse, yanking that off. *Good lord!* His cock was hard and peeking out the top of his low-riding jeans. Making her mouth water and her pussy clench all at the same time.

Gage unsnapped her bra, immediately dipping his head so that he could nip at her nipples. Oh, that mouth, his teeth, his wicked tongue. Edith moaned.

Gage rubbed her through her underwear. Zoning in on her clit through the material. It felt good. She moaned again, feeling her body ready itself for him. Excitement coursed through her. "You lose the pantyhose and the underwear while I fetch a condom." He gestured towards the bedroom. His voice was thick with desire. A deep rasp of need.

Edith shook her head. "We don't need to use a

condom."

"What?" His head shot up, his eyes locking with hers.

Edith shook her head. "I've been back on the pill for a full cycle so…" She looked him in the eyes.

"You realize that no birth control is foolproof?" He raised his brows. "Not even my nose."

"I know. I've never had sex without a condom before."

"You know my take on this, on us." He gave her a sweet half-smile. "I'm all in, Curls. Hopefully, literally as well as figuratively."

"I know," she shrugged, "and I'm ready to take this step."

His eyes widened and brightened. "I get to come inside you?" He didn't wait for a reply, Gage picked her up and began to walk. There was a ripping sound. Goodbye pantyhose. There was another tug and he was placing her on the edge of the kitchen counter. Goodbye lace panties. Edith wrapped her legs around him. When had he opened his jeans? They were hanging halfway down his thighs, his cock proud and ready.

Then he was lining up and driving into her. One hard thrust put him balls deep. Gage growled and her mind turned mushy. Her whole body came alive. "You feel amazing, Curls." His eyes drifted shut. The skin of his face pulled tight and his jaw clenched. "So damned good."

Edith was panting. "You do too," she pushed out.

"You have to agree to this. To us. I want to wake up with you every day." He eased out before pushing back in. "Sleep with you every night." He held onto her, holding her in place, changing the angle. "I want you, only you, I want this." His thrusts were harder, more intense. Hitting every spot inside her. It was them, skin to skin. No holding back this time. No stopping.

Edith couldn't talk, she could only feel. That and breathe. Hard pants that filled the still mostly empty house. Pants that quickly turned to moans and moans to yells.

Then she was throwing her head back and screaming as her orgasm took her. Carrying her higher and higher. "Yes," she yelled as Gage tensed, bending slightly over the middle, his fingers digging in deeper, his movements becoming jerky. He groaned. She could feel him come inside her in hot bursts. He was pulling her close and breathing her in as he found his completion. It felt real. It felt right. It felt like everything fell into place.

He was breathing heavily. Still deep inside her. His head in the crook of her neck. "I can't wait to bite you."

She laughed. "That's not very nice." She still sounded out of breath.

"Oh..." Gage nipped at her neck and her pussy clenched. Edith sucked in a ragged breath. "I think you might like it very much." He nipped her again and she moaned.

"That feels so good." She pulled back so that she could look into his eyes. "That *yes* I yelled earlier…"

Gage kissed her. He made a sound of acknowledgment.

"Well, it was my answer."

Gage pulled back his eyes wide. "You'll move in with me?"

Edith nodded. "Of course I'll move in with you."

"Oh, Curls." Gage pulled her in close for a hug. "You have no idea how happy I am."

"I think I might have an inkling," she said on a smile.

AUTHOR'S NOTE

Charlene Hartnady is a USA Today Bestselling author. She loves to write about all things paranormal including vampires, elves and shifters of all kinds. Charlene lives on an acre in the country with her gorgeous husband and three sons. They have an array of pets including a couple of horses.

She is lucky enough to be able to write full time, so most days you can find her at her computer writing up a storm. Charlene believes that it is the small things that truly matter like that feeling you get when you start a new book, or a particularly beautiful sunset.

BOOKS BY THIS AUTHOR

The Chosen Series:

Book 1 ~ Chosen by the Vampire Kings
Book 2 ~ Stolen by the Alpha Wolf
Book 3 ~ Unlikely Mates
Book 4 ~ Awakened by the Vampire Prince
Book 5 ~ Mated to the Vampire Kings (Short Novel)
Book 6 ~ Wolf Whisperer (Novella)
Book 7 ~ Wanted by the Elven King

Demon Chaser Series (No cliffhangers):

Book 1 ~ Omega
Book 2 ~ Alpha
Book 3 ~ Hybrid
Book 4 ~ Skin
Demon Chaser Boxed Set Book 1–3

BOOKS BY THIS AUTHOR

The Program Series (Vampire Novels):
Book 1 ~ A Mate for York
Book 2 ~ A Mate for Gideon
Book 3 ~ A Mate for Lazarus
Book 4 ~ A Mate for Griffin
Book 5 ~ A Mate for Lance
Book 6 ~ A Mate for Kai
Book 7 ~ A Mate for Titan

The Bride Hunt Series (Dragon Shifter Novels):
Book 1 ~ Royal Dragon
Book 2 ~ Water Dragon
Book 3 ~ Dragon King
Book 4 ~ Lightning Dragon
Book 5 ~ Forbidden Dragon
Book 6 ~ Dragon Prince

A MATE FOR YORK

The Program Book 1

CHARLENE HARTNADY

1

C ASSIDY'S HANDS WERE CLAMMY and shaking. She had just retyped the same thing three times. At this rate, she would have to work even later than normal to get her work done. She sighed heavily.

Pull yourself together.

With shaking hands, she grabbed her purse from the floor next to her, reached inside and pulled out the folded up newspaper article.

Have you ever wanted to date a vampire?

Human women required. Must be enthusiastic about interactions with vampires. Must be willing to undergo a stringent medical exam. Must be prepared to sign a *contractual agreement which would include a non-disclosure clause. This will be a temporary position. Limited spaces available within the program. Successful candidates can earn up to $45,000 per day, over a three-day period.*

All she needed was three days leave.

Cassidy wasn't sure whether her hands were shaking because she had to ask for the leave and her boss was a total douche bag or because the thought of vampires drinking her blood wasn't exactly a welcome one.

More than likely a combination of both.

This was a major opportunity for her though. She had already been accepted into the trial phase of the program that the vampires were running. What was three days in her life? So there was a little risk involved. Okay, a lot of risk, but it would all be worth it in the end. She was drowning in debt. Stuck in a dead-end job. Stuck in this godforsaken town. This was her chance, her golden opportunity, and she planned on seizing it with both hands.

To remind herself what she was working towards, or at least running away from, she let her eyes roam around her cluttered desk. There were several piles of documents needing to be filed. A stack of orders lay next to her cranky old laptop. Hopefully it wouldn't freeze on her this time while she was uploading them into the system. It had been months since Sarah had left. There used to be two of them performing her job, and since her colleague was never replaced it was just her. She increasingly found that she had to get to work way earlier and stay later and later just to get the job done.

To add insult to injury, there were many days that her

a-hole boss still had the audacity to come down on her for not meeting a deadline. He refused to listen to reason and would not accept being understaffed as an excuse. She'd never been one to shy away from hard work but the expectations were ridiculous. Her only saving grace was that she didn't have much of a life.

There had to be something more out there for her – and a hundred and thirty-five thousand big ones would not only pay off her debts but would also give her enough cash to go out and find one. A life, that is, and a damned good life it would be.

Cassidy took a deep breath and squared her shoulders. If she asked really nicely, hopefully Mark would give her a couple of days off. She couldn't remember the last time she had taken leave. Then it dawned on her, she'd taken three days after Sean had died a year ago. Her boss couldn't say no though. If he did, she wasn't beyond begging.

Rising to her feet, she made for the closed door at the other end of her office. After knocking twice, she entered.

The lazy ass was spread out on the corner sofa with his hands crossed behind his head. He didn't look in the least bit embarrassed about her finding him like that either.

"Cassidy." He put on a big cheesy smile as he rose to a sitting position. The buttons on his jacket pulled tight around his paunchy midsection. He didn't move much and ate big greasy lunches so it wasn't surprising. "Come on in. Take a seat," he gestured to a spot next to him on the sofa.

That would be the day. Her boss could get a bit touchy feely. Thankfully it had never gone beyond a pat on the

CHARLENE HARTNADY

butt, a hand on her shoulder or just a general invasion of her personal space. It put her on edge though because it was becoming worse of late. The sexual innuendos were also getting highly irritating. She pretended that they went over her head, but he was becoming more and more forward as time went by.

By the way his eyes moved down her body, she could tell that he was most definitely mentally undressing her. *Oh god.* That meant that he was in one of his grabby moods. *Damn.* She preferred it when he was acting like a total jerk. Easier to deal with.

"No, that's fine. Thank you." She worked hard to plaster a smile on her face. "I don't want to take up much of your time and I have to get back to work myself."

His eyes narrowed for a second before dropping to her breasts. "You could do with a little break every now and then… so could I for that matter." Even though she knew he couldn't see anything because of her baggy jacket, his eyes stayed glued to her boobs anyway. Why did she get the distinct impression that he was no longer talking about work? *Argh!*

"How long has your husband been gone now?" he asked, his gaze still locked on her chest. It made her want to fold her arms but she resisted the temptation.

None of your damned business.

"It's been a year now since Sean passed." She tried hard to look sad and mournful. The truth was, if the bastard wasn't already dead she would've killed him herself. Turned out that there were things about Sean that she hadn't known. In fact, it was safe to say that she'd been living with and married to a total stranger. Funny how those things tended to come out when a person died.

Her boss did not need to know this information though. So far, playing the mourning wife was the only thing that kept him from pursuing her further.

"What can I do for you?" His eyes slid down to the juncture at her thighs and she had to fight the urge to squeeze them tightly together. Even though temperatures outside were damn near scorching, she still wore stockings, skirt to mid-calf, a button-up blouse and a jacket. Nothing was revealing and yet he still looked at her like she was standing there naked. It made her skin crawl. "I would be happy to oblige you. Just say the word, baby."

She hated it when he called her that. He started doing it a couple of weeks ago. Cassidy had asked him on several occasions to stop but she may as well have been speaking to a plank of wood.

She grit her teeth for a second, holding back a retort. "Great. Glad to hear it." Her voice sounded way more confident than she felt. "I need a couple of days off. It's been a really long time—"

"Forget it," he interrupted while standing up. "I need you… here." Another innuendo. Although she waited, he didn't give any further explanations.

"Look, I know there is a lot to do around here especially since Sarah left." His eyes clouded over immediately at the mention of her ex-colleague's name. "I would be happy to put in extra time."

As in, she wouldn't sleep and would have to work weekends to get the job done.

"I'll do whatever it takes. I just really need a couple of days. It's important."

His eyes lit up and she realized what she had just said and how it would've sounded to a complete pig like Mark.

"Anything?" he rolled the word off of his tongue.

"Well…" It came out sounding breathless but only because she was nervous. "Not anything. What I meant to say was—"

"No, no. I like that you would do anything, in fact, there is something I've been meaning to discuss with you." His gaze dropped to her breasts again.

Please no. Anything but that.

Cassidy swallowed hard, actually feeling sick to her stomach. She shook her head.

"You can have a few days, baby. In fact, I'll hire you an assistant." Ironically he played with the wedding band on his ring finger. His voice had turned sickly sweet. "I'd be willing to go a long way for you if you only met me halfway. It's time you got over the loss of your husband and I plan on helping you to do that."

"Um… I don't think…" Her voice was soft and shaky. Her hands shook too, so she folded her arms.

This was not happening.

"Look, Cass… baby, you're an okay-looking woman. Not normally the type I'd go for. I prefer them a bit younger, bigger tits, tighter ass…" He looked her up and down as if he were sizing her up and finding her lacking. "I'd be willing to give you a go… help you out. Now… baby…" he paused.

Cassidy felt like the air had seized in her lungs, like her heart had stopped beating. Her mouth gaped open but she couldn't close it. She tried to speak but could only manage a croak.

She watched in horror as her boss pulled down his zipper and pulled out a wrinkled, flaccid cock. "Suck on this. Or you could bend over and I'll fuck you – the choice is yours. I would recommend the fuck because quite frankly I think you could use it." He was deadly serious. Even gave a small nod like he was doing her a favor or something.

To the delight of her oxygen starved lungs, she managed to suck in a deep breath but still couldn't get any words out. Not a single, solitary syllable.

"I know you've had to play the part of the devastated wife and all that but I'm sure you really want a bit of this." He waved his cock at her, although wave was not the right description. The problem was that a limp dick couldn't really wave. It flopped about pathetically in his hand.

Cassidy looked from his tiny dick up to his ruddy, pasty face and back down again before bursting out laughing. It was the kind of laugh that had her bending at the knees, hunching over. Sucking in another lungful of air, she gave it all she had. Unable to stop even if she wanted to. Until tears rolled down her cheeks. Until she was gasping for breath.

"Hey now…" Mark started to look distinctly uncomfortable. "That's not really the sort of response I expected from you." He didn't look so sure anymore, even started to put his dick away before his eyes hardened.

Cassidy wiped the tears from her face. She still couldn't believe what the hell she was seeing and even worse, what she was hearing. *What a complete asshole.*

Her boss took a step towards her. "The time for games

is over. Get down on your knees if you want to keep your job. I'm your boss and your behavior is just plain rude."

Any hint of humor evaporated in an instant. "I'll tell you what's rude… you taking out your thing is rude. You're right, you're my boss which means what is happening right here," she gestured between the two of them, looking pointedly at his member, "is called sexual harassment."

He narrowed his eyes at her. "Damn fucking straight, little missy. I want you to sexually harass this right now." He clutched his penis, flopping it around some more.

"Alrighty then. Let me just go and fetch my purse," she grinned at him, putting every little bit of sarcasm she had into the smile.

"Why would you need your purse?" he frowned.

"To get my magnifying glass. You have just about the smallest dick that I've ever seen." Not that she had seen many, but she didn't think she needed to. His penis was a joke.

It was his turn to gape. To turn a shade of bright red. "You didn't just say that. I'm going to pretend that I didn't hear that. This is your last fucking chance." Spittle flew from his mouth. "Show me your tits and get onto your fucking knees. Make me fucking come and do it now or you are out of a job."

"You can pretend all you want. As far as I'm concerned you can pretend that I'm sucking on your limp dick as well, because it will never happen. You can take your job and your tiny penis and shove um where the sun don't shine!" Cassidy almost wanted to slap a hand over her mouth, she couldn't believe that she had just said all of that. One thing was for sure, she was done taking shit from men. *Done!*

She gave him a disgusted look, turned on her heel and walked out. After grabbing her purse, she left without looking back, praying that her old faithful car would start. It hadn't been serviced since before her husband had died and it wasn't sounding right lately. The gearbox grated sometimes when she changed gears. There was a rattling noise. She just didn't have the funds. That was all about to change though. She hadn't exactly planned on leaving her job just yet. What if things didn't work out? She'd planned on keeping her job as a safety net instead of counting chickens she didn't have. It was too late to go back now.

Despite her lack of a backup plan, Cassidy grinned as her car started with a rattle and a splutter. Grinned even wider as she pulled away, hearing the gravel crunch beneath her tires. Now all she had to do was get through the next few days and she was home free.

A Mate for York is available now.

Printed in Poland
by Amazon Fulfillment
Poland Sp. z o.o., Wrocław